THE VILLAGE BY THE RIVER

H. LOUISA BEDFORD

1st WORLD
LIBRARY
Literary Society

The Village by the River

H. Louisa Bedford

© 1st World Library, 2009
PO Box 2211
Fairfield, IA 52556
www.1stworldlibrary.com
First Edition

LCCN: 2009923396

Softcover ISBN: 978-1-4218-8843-9
Hardcover ISBN: 978-1-4218-8942-9
eBook ISBN: 978-1-4218-8744-9

Purchase *"The Village by the River"*
as a traditional bound book at:
www.1stWorldLibrary.com/purchase.asp?ISBN=978-1-4218-8843-9

1st World Library is a literary, educational organization
dedicated to:

- Creating a free internet library of downloadable ebooks

- Hosting writing competitions and offering book publishing
scholarships.

1ˢᵗ World Library Literary Society

Giving Back to the World

"If you want to work on the core problem, it's early school literacy."

- James Barksdale, former CEO of Netscape

"No skill is more crucial to the future of a child, or to a democratic and prosperous society, than literacy."

- Los Angeles Times

"Literacy... means far more than learning how to read and write... The aim is to transmit... knowledge and promote social participation."

- UNESCO

"Literacy is not a luxury, it is a right and a responsibility. If our world is to meet the challenges of the twenty-first century we must harness the energy and creativity of all our citizens."

- President Bill Clinton

"Parents should be encouraged to read to their children, and teachers should be equipped with all available techniques for teaching literacy, so the varying needs and capacities of individual kids can be taken into account."

- Hugh Mackay

CONTENTS

CHAPTER I

WHAT THE VILLAGERS SAID

"Well, it were the grandest funeral as ever I set eyes on," said Allison, the blacksmith, folding his brawny arms under his leather apron, and leaning his shoulders against the open door of the smithy in an attitude of leisurely ease.

The group, gathered round him on their way home from work, gave an assenting nod and waited for more.

For convenience Allison shifted his pipe more to the corner of his mouth, and proceeded—

"Not one of yer new-fangled ones, with a glass hearse for all the world like a big window-box, and a sight of white flowers like a wedding. Everything was as black as it should be; I never see'd finer horses, in my life, with manes and tails reachin' a'most to the ground, and a shinin' black hearse with a score of plumes on the top, and half a dozen men with silk hatbands walking alongside it, right away from the station to the churchyard yonder." And Allison threw a backward glance over the billowy golden cornfields, which separated the village from the church by a quarter of a mile, where the grand tower reared its head as if keeping watch over the village like a lofty sentinel.

"There were lots of follerers, I expect?" suggested Macdonald, gently. He was a Scotchman, and worked on the line, and he shifted his bag of tools from his shoulder to the ground as he spoke. "A gentleman like him would leave a-many to miss him."

Allison stared across at the river which ran swiftly by on the opposite side of the road. The long village of Rudham skirted its banks irregularly for a mile or more. The blacksmith had plenty of news to communicate, but he was not to be hurried in the relating of it.

"I'm tryin' to recolleck," he said, knitting his brows, "but I can't mind more than two principal mourners. And the undertaker, when he stopped to water his horses at the inn, told Mrs. Lake as they was the doctor and the lawyer; but, relations or no, they did it wonderful well! Stood with their hats off all in the burnin' sun, and went back to look at the grave when the funeral was over."

"The household servants was there—leastways the butler and footman," said Tom Burney, a dark-eyed, gipsy-looking young man, who was one of the under-gardeners at the big house on the hill, "but not him as is coming after."

"The question is who is a-comin' after?" said Allison, in a tone of sarcastic argument. "Maybe you'll tell us, as you seem to know such a lot about it?"

Burney coloured under his dark skin, and gave an uneasy little laugh.

"I know what I've heard, no more nor less," he said; "but it comes first-hand from the butler of him who's gone."

Allison gave an incredulous sniff; he was not used to playing

H. Louisa Bedford

second fiddle, and the heads of his listeners had turned to a man in the direction of the last speaker.

"He hadn't no near relation, not bein' a married man," went on Burney, enjoying his advantage; "and Mr. Smith—that's the butler—came and walked round the garden until it was time for his train to go back to London."

"He don't pretend as the property's left to him, I suppose?" broke in Allison, jocosely.

Burney turned his shoulder slightly towards the speaker, and went on, regardless of the interruption—

"Mr. Smith says as the house up there, and all the property, goes to a young fellow not more than thirty, of the same name as the old squire; some third cousin or other."

"Hearsay! just hearsay!" ejaculated Allison, contemptuously. "Who's seen him, I should like to know? Seein's believin', they say."

"Mr. Smith has," said Burney, a ring of triumph in his voice. "He were there when old Mr. Lessing died."

There was silence for a moment. The evidence seemed conclusive, and Allison's discomfiture complete; but, as the forge was the place where the village gossips gathered every day, it was felt to be wise to keep on good terms with the owner.

"Seems as if it might be true," said Macdonald, casting a timid glance at the blacksmith.

"If it is, why wern't he here, to-day, then?" asked Allison, gruffly.

"Not knowin', can't say," Burney answered with a laugh.

"Maybe he'll be comin' to live here," said another.

"He can't! I can tell you that much; there ain't a house he could live in," asserted Allison. "His own place is let, you see, to the Websters—whom Burney there works for,—and he can't turn 'em out, as they have it on lease; and a good thing too. We don't want no resident squire ridin' round and pryin' into everything. The old one kept hisself to hisself, and, as long as the rents was paid regular, he didn't trouble much about us; and there was always a pound for the widows every Christmas. Trust me, it's better to have your landlord livin' in London, and not looking about the place more than once a year. Did Mr. Smith say what the young one looked like, Burney?"

The question was asked a little reluctantly.

"No; but he thinks he's a bit queer in his notions. He asked him whether he'd be likely to want his services; and Mr. Lessing laughed quite loud, and said, one nice old woman to cook and do for him was all he should require now, or at any time in his life. Mr. Smith ain't sure but what he's a Socialist."

"I don't rightly know the meaning of it?" said Macdonald, instinctively, turning to the blacksmith for an explanation.

"It may be a good thing, or it mayn't," declared Allison. "I take it that a Socialist means one as would take from those as has plenty and give to those who has nothing. We're born ekal into the world, and they'd keep us ekal, as far as might be. But it'd take a deal of workin' out, more than you'd think, lookin' at it first; but I'm not goin' to say that it wouldn't be handy to have a Socialist squire. He might divide his land

H. Louisa Bedford

ekal among us, and there'd be no more rent to pay for any of us. There now!"

A general murmur of approval ran round his audience, except with old Macdonald, who gave a quaint smile.

"But it strikes me that such of us as have saved a tidy bit would have to hand it out to be divided equal too. It would not be fair as the Squire should do it all; it would run through, you see."

"Well, I've not saved a brass farthing, so I should come in for a lot; and I'd settle down and marry to-morrow!" cried Burney, gaily. "But, you may depend on it, whoever's got the place will stick to it. I must be getting on to the station. Our people are coming back from abroad this evening, and I'm to be there to help hoist up the luggage. It takes a carriage and pair to carry up the ladies, and an extra cart for luggage."

"It's not the luggage you're going to meet, I'll bet; it's the lady's maid," said a young fellow, who had not spoken before. "If you married next week we all know well enough whom you'd take for a wife;" and Tom moved off amid a shout of laughter.

It was an open secret that Tom was head-over-ears in love with pretty Rose Lancaster, the somewhat flighty maid of Miss Webster, who, with her mother, was returning to the Court that evening. Absence had made his heart grow fonder, and it was beating much faster than usual as he stood on the station platform awaiting the arrival of the train, and, when it ran in with much splutter and fuss, not even by a turn of her head did Miss Rose show herself aware of Tom's presence. Instead, she was looking after her ladies, lifting out their various belongings—not a few in number—and ordering round the porters with a pretty pertness as she counted out the boxes from the van. It was only when she found her own box missing that she turned appealingly to Tom.

"Run, there's a good boy, quick to the other van!" she said, acknowledging him with a nod. "It must have got in there, and the train will be off in another moment."

Tom ran as requested, pantingly rescued the box, and came back smiling to tell her of his successful search.

"That's right," said Rose, graciously. "Now you can help me on to the box-seat of the carriage, if you like. I'm going to sit beside Mr. Dixon."

Dixon was the coachman, and a formidable rival in Tom's eyes.

"I thought, perhaps, as you'd come along of me. I'm drivin' the cart back for Berry, as he had a message in the village. I've not seen you for such a time, Rose."

"Come with you!" said Rose, with a toss of her head. "The ladies would not like it; besides, we shall meet sure enough some day soon. I mustn't wait a minute longer. You need not help me unless you like."

But poor Tom, under the pretext of making some inquiry about the luggage, managed to be near so as to hand up Rose to her seat by the coachman, who appeared far more absorbed in the management of his horses than in the young woman who sat by him, upon whom he did not bestow even a glance, preserving a perfectly imperturbable countenance.

"He's pretending! just pretending—the scamp!" said Tom, under his breath, turning back to his horse and cart.

H. Louisa Bedford

A strange man stood near stroking the animal's head and keeping a light hand on its bridle. He wore a loosely fitting brown suit, and the hand that caressed the horse was almost as brown as his clothes. His head was closely cropped and his face clean-shaven, showing the clear-cut, decided mouth and chin, and the white, even teeth displayed by the smile with which he greeted Tom.

"You may be glad I was at hand or your cart with its cargo of luggage would have been upset in the road," he said. "It's not a wise thing to leave a creature like this standing alone when a train is starting off."

A quick retort was on the tip of Tom's tongue; he had no fancy for being called to account by a perfect stranger, but, although the words sounded authoritative, the tone was good-humoured.

"Thank you, I only left him for a moment; he stands quiet enough as a rule," he said, taking the bridle into his hand.

The stranger picked up the small portmanteau he had set down in the road, and prepared to walk off, then turned half-hesitatingly back to Tom.

"Can you tell me where I can get a night or two's lodging? It does not much matter where it is as long as it is clean and quiet."

Tom took off his cap and rubbed his head thoughtfully.

"Mrs. Lake's a wonderful good sort of woman."

"And who may Mrs. Lake be?" inquired the stranger, pleasantly.

"She keeps the Blue Dragon, but I couldn't say as it's exactly quiet of a Saturday night. She don't allow no swearin' on her premises, but some of the fellers gets a bit rowdy before they go home."

"Very possibly," replied his companion, dryly. "I don't think the Blue Dragon would suit me; but surely there is some cottager with a spare bed and sitting-room, who might be glad of a quiet, respectable lodger for a bit?"

Tom threw a searching glance at the speaker; he was not quite sure that, notwithstanding his gentle manner of talking, he was to be altogether trusted.

"If you'd step up beside me I'll drive you to the forge," he said, willing to shelve his responsibility of recommendation. "It's close here, and Allison will help you if no one else can. He knows every one's business."

"Just the sort of man I want," said Tom's new acquaintance, climbing into the cart and seating himself on the cushion that had been intended for Rose. His alert grey eyes took in his new surroundings at a glance.

No one could call Rudham a pretty village: it was too straggling, too bare of trees, which had been planted sparsely and attained no luxuriance of growth; but it was not wholly unattractive this evening, with the setting sun turning to gold the varying bends of the river which ran through the valley, and the cottages and farmhouses dotted here and there with a not unpleasing irregularity, and in the distance a softly rising upland turning from blue to purple in the evening light.

"Yonder's the Court, where my people live," said Tom, jerking his whip to a big house more than a mile away that peeped out from among the trees. "It belonged to the old squire who was buried to-day, you know."

"Ah!" ejaculated his listener, not greatly interested, apparently, in the information.

"It's a wonderful fine place, and they say as he who's to have it won't hold no store by it. Pity, ain't it?"

Tom's companion broke into rather a disconcerting laugh.

"Look here, my lad, by the time you're thirty you won't give credit to every bit of gossip that comes to your ears; you'll wait to know that it's true before you pass it on, at any rate. This will be the forge you spoke of, and there's the owner, sure enough, standing at the door. Thank you for the lift, and here's a shilling for your trouble."

But Tom thrust away the proffered tip with a shake of his head.

"No, thank you; you kept the horse safe at the station."

"So, on the principle that one good turn deserves another, you'll give me a lift for nothing. All right and thank you," said the man, dismounting and lifting out his portmanteau. "Good night."

"Good night," said Tom, with an answering nod. "I wonder what his business is?" he thought, as he pursued his way. "Shouldn't be surprised if he was the engineer who's to see to the laying down of the new line; he's that quick, smart way with him as if he'd been about a lot and knew a thing or two."

"Lodgings!" echoed Allison, slowly, as the stranger reiterated his request. "It's not a thing we are often asked for in Rudham. I'd make no objection to taking you in myself, but Mrs. Allison's not partial to strangers."

"I should be sorry to inconvenience Mrs. Allison; is there no one else you can think of?"

"Mrs. Pink 'ud do it; but she's a baby who's teething, and fretful o' nights."

"And that would not suit me!" said the newcomer, with decision.

"I have it!" cried Allison, bringing down his big hand with a resounding slap upon his knee. "Mrs. Macdonald's the body for you! There's not a better woman in Rudham, and I know 'em pretty well in these parts. Her husband's only just gone up street; he were talkin' here not five minutes ago. There's only their two selves, and the cottage one of the best in the place."

"It sounds as if it would suit me down to the ground. And if Mrs. Macdonald could give me shelter, even for a few nights, it would give me time to look about me."

"Thinkin' of settlin' in these parts?" inquired Allison. "There's no house as I knows on vacant."

"I've no settled plans at present," answered the stranger. "If you'll kindly direct me to Mrs. Macdonald's, I'll go and try my fate."

"Eighth house from here, set back a bit from the road, with a little orchard behind it; and you can say as I sent you," said Allison, feeling his name a good enough recommendation for any stranger.

The door of the eighth house set back a little from the road was partially open as the new arrival made his way up the box-bordered path, with beds on either side of it gay with flowers; and before he could knock a neatly dressed middle-aged woman threw it wide and surveyed him from head to foot.

"And what may you be wanting, sir?" she asked, quite civilly.

"A lodging for a night or two. And Mr. Allison at the forge seemed to think you might be inclined to take me in."

"I'm not sure as my John will wish it. But if you'll step inside I'll ask him," replied Mrs. Macdonald, motioning him to a chair.

"Unless they turn me out by force, I shall stay," he said, looking round him with a pleased smile.

It was not his fault, but "my John's" deafness, that caused him to hear himself described as a "very decent man, who spoke as civil as a gentleman; and it was awkward to find yourself in a strange place on a Saturday night with nobody ready to put themselves about a bit to take you in."

"John will yield in the long run," sighed the unwilling listener. "Mrs. MacD. rules the roost, unless I'm greatly mistaken."

Apparently his conjecture was right, for in another minute the woman reappeared to say that she and her husband were willing to let him have the front bed and sitting-room if, after due inspection, they proved good enough for him.

"We're not used to grand folk," she said, a trifle awed by the sight of the portmanteau. "I cooked for a plain family before I married my John, and—"

"Then it's certain that you can cook for me; I'm not nearly so much trouble as a plain family," said her visitor, laughing. "I'll carry up my things if you'll show me the way, for I shall go no further than this to-night. I dare say you can give me some tea, and then I'll go out and order in some food."

"I dare say you eat hearty, sir; or we've some fine new-laid eggs," suggested Mrs. Macdonald.

"The very thing. You can't get such a thing in London; the youngest new-laid egg is about a month old, I fancy. Thank you," (with a glance round the dimity-curtained room, fragrant with lavender); "I shall be as happy as a king."

When her lodger was safely established at his evening meal, and Mrs. Macdonald was satisfied that she could provide nothing more for his comfort, she went upstairs to tidy his room, shaking her head a little over the various things that littered the floor and table.

"He's not so tidy as my John, but he's not got his years over his head," she said, as she closed the portmanteau and shoved it towards the dressing-room table.

As she did so the name on the label caught her eye, she could not help reading it; and then drew in her breath with a sharp exclamation of surprise. The next instant she hurried softly but quickly down the stairs, took her astonished helpmeet by the arm, and dragged him into the orchard, closing the kitchen door behind her.

"John!" she said, "who do you think has come to us? Who is it that has come quite humble like for shelter under our roof this night?"

In her eagerness to extract an answer she pinched the arm she held a little.

"It's not a riddle you're asking me?" said John, withdrawing himself a pace.

"No, no, man! it's the young squire himself, for sure. Paul Lessing is on his portmanter," she said looking round, for fear she should be overheard by a neighbour. The news must be digested.

CHAPTER II

AN UNLOOKED-FOR INHERITANCE

A week before, Paul Lessing and his only sister Sally had started for a three week's tour on the continent, with as light-hearted a sense of enjoyment as any boy or girl home for the summer vacation. They were orphans, with only each other to care for; and Paul had not feared to take up some of their slender capital to enable his sister to complete her college course at Girton. If she had to earn her own living, she should at least have the best education that money could give; and Sally had made the best use of her opportunity. Her name was high in the honour list, and Paul decreed that, before any plans were discussed for her future, they should dedicate a certain sum to a foreign tour.

"It will be a good investment, Sally. You are looking pale after all your work. We will make no definite plan; it's distance that swallows up the money, so we'll start off for Brussels, and move on when we feel inclined, possibly to the Rhine, and so to Heidelberg." And Sally, in the joyousness of her mood, felt that all places would be alike delightful in the company of her brother.

Two days later found the brother and sister seated in the garden of the *cafe* that adjoins the park at Brussels. Even

H. Louisa Bedford

now, at eight o'clock in the evening, it was exceedingly hot, and the boughs of the trees overhead, through which here and there a star glimmered, were absolutely motionless. The band which played was the best string-band in Brussels, attracting a great throng of listeners; and every table around them had its complement of guests; and the civil waiters who flitted hither and thither had almost more than they could do to keep the tables properly served. Paul was smoking and reading the paper, but Sally needed no better amusement than to watch the various groups about her, and to listen to the exquisite playing of the band.

"We want something like this in England, Paul," she said, laying a hand on his arm—"lots of places like this out-of-doors in the fresh air, under the stars and trees, where people can go and drink their tea or coffee, and listen to music that must refine them whilst they listen."

Paul laid by his paper and laughed. "Yes," he said, "and when I get into Parliament—if ever—I will do my utmost to make some of our wealthy citizens disgorge a part of their wealth to put places such as this within the reach of everybody. I confess there are difficulties—"

"What?" inquired Sally, with childish impatience.

"Our beastly climate, to begin with," Paul answered with a little laugh. "Want of space, and want of trees when you get the space. Then look at our population in our big cities. Brussels is just a pocket-town, if you come to compare it with London. Of course the recreation of the masses is only one of the many vexed questions concerning them that Government eventually must take in hand. If you want people to be moral, you must give them a chance of enjoying themselves in an innocent fashion."

"Of course, you could do a lot if you once got into Parliament!" cried Sally, with the enthusiasm of her twenty years. "When shall you get in? and where shall you stand for? and may I help in the election?"

Paul laughed louder than before. "There's a deal to be done before I can even think of standing for any place. First, I must accumulate enough capital to bring me in a small independent income. You know we have not much now."

"You can have anything and everything that belongs to me; I mean to earn my living somehow," declared Sally, sturdily.

"Thank you. I don't mean to start that way; and money comes in slowly to a barrister, although I am getting on fairly well. Then I will stand for any place that will return me, after learning my honestly expressed political opinions. Each man has his pet hobby, and I feel that mine is the bettering of the condition of the masses."

"That will make you popular," said Sally.

"And I don't care a fig for popularity. I want to help to leave the average condition of the people better than it is at present. The contrast between the very rich and the very poor of our land is something too awful to contemplate."

His talk, which he had begun half in play, had ended in deadly earnest; and Sally laid her hand mischievously over his eyes.

"Then don't contemplate it—at any rate just now, when I am so merry and happy. You've not answered my last question. May I help in your election? It would be such fun."

"I think not, Sally," Paul said smiling again.

"Oh, what a mass of inconsistency!—when you were saying only to-day that you saw no just cause or impediment why women should not do anything for which they have a special fitness. Now I feel politics will be my speciality, and I would not canvass for any one unless I quite understood their views."

"Well, my Parliamentary career is in the far future," Paul interposed; "and certainly I should not give my sanction to your undertaking any work of that kind at present. You are much too young, and much too—"

"Pretty, were you going to add?" broke in Sally, with a ripple of laughter. "I'm afraid not: enthusiastic would be the more likely adjective for you to use concerning me. Besides I don't think I am pretty. 'My dear,' said that candid old Miss Sykes to me the other day, 'you might have been very good-looking if all your features were as good as your eyes.' Why do ladies of a certain age take it for granted that they can say what they choose to the budding young woman? It annoys me frightfully. Oh, Paul!" with a sudden lowering of her voice, "talking of pretty, there's a perfectly lovely girl who is seated with her mother at the third table from ours. Don't turn your head too quickly or she will think we are talking of her; and then you can keep your head turned in the direction of the band. Her profile comes in between it and you."

Paul did as he was bid. Sally was right, the girl to whom she directed his attention was lovely beyond compare; and yet there was something in her face that failed to satisfy him. The very perfection, too, of everything about her, gave him a feeling of unconscious irritation.

"Well?" asked Sally, when he turned back to her.

"She's beautiful, certainly; but I don't like her."

"It's just because you did not discover her first."

Paul did not trouble to answer; there was a general stir amongst the company. The concert was drawing to a close, and the burghers of Brussels began to think of home and bed. The wives slipped their knitting into their pocket; the husbands bestowed a passing nod and guttural good night to each other as they moved away; and the twinkling lights began to be extinguished one by one. In the crowd at the entrance Paul and Sally found themselves close to the girl whom Sally had so greatly admired. She was talking in low, clear tones to her mother.

"Ought not to have come? What nonsense, mother! It has been quite an amusing experience to see the way these people pass their evenings; they are quite nice and respectable. I confess now I should be glad to see our carriage. I feel I'm getting smoke-dried like bacon—or ham, is it?"

It was evident that the elder of the two ladies was rather frightened and losing her head.

"I'll not do this again without a man of our own," she said with nervous irritability.

Paul stepped forward, raising his hat. "Is your carriage anywhere about? Can I get it for you?"

"Oh, thank you so much. It's a private one from the Hotel de Flandres, and I told the man to stop here."

"Unfortunately the police regulations interfere with your orders," Paul said, with a slight smile. "He must take his place in the ranks. I will soon find it for you if you will stay here."

H. Louisa Bedford

"Name, Webster," said the older lady.

So Paul, with a nod to Sally to stay where she was, hurried off, returning in a moment with the carriage.

"Thanks so much," said the girl whom Sally admired, as Paul handed her in and closed the door behind her.

"I was quite glad of the time to consider her more closely!" cried Sally, as they drove off. "I've never seen what I call an absolutely perfect face before. I wonder if I shall see her again?"

"For my part I don't wish it," Paul answered carelessly. "Beautiful she is; but she bears the knowledge of it about with her like an overpowering perfume, and is the very impersonation of the insolence of riches!"

"Why, Paul, you are not often either narrow-minded or unjust."

"How dare she comment upon these Belgians, who nearly all possess a smattering of English, under their very noses!" continued Paul, angrily. "'Quite nice and respectable,' indeed! As she and her mother were in a fix I was bound, as a man, to offer my services; but I did it unwillingly."

Paul's indignation was short-lived, and he and Sally walked along the streets leisurely, on their way back to their hotel, talking on indifferent subjects. They paused in the hall of the hotel, running their eyes over the letters displayed outside the post-office, to see if the evening post had brought any for them. There were none for Sally; but two or three for Paul, that had been forwarded from his chambers in London.

"I'll go into the salon and read them, and then we'll go

upstairs to bed. I feel infected by the early hours of these foreigners," he said, yawning a little.

Sally turned over the leaves of a paper whilst her brother opened his letters. The last of them he read and re-read several times; then rose and laid his hand on Sally's shoulder.

"I'm awfully sorry, Sally, but I shall have to go back to London by the first train to-morrow."

The long-drawn "O-o-o-h!" was powerless to express half the disappointment his sister felt.

"It's business, I suppose: everything nasty is always business," she said at last.

"Well, no, it's not business; and it certainly is not pleasure. You remember I had an old godfather, Major Lessing? I'm sure he amply fulfilled his godfatherly duty by the silver milk-jug he gave me at my baptism—which I've never set eyes on for many a long year, by the way—and the tips he shoved into the palm of my hand whenever I paid him a visit on my way from school. I don't think I've seen him since; and why, now that he's dying, he has a particular desire for a call, I can't tell you. It's inconvenient, to say the least of it."

"*Must* you go?" asked Sally, despairingly.

"I'm afraid so. It's the last thing one can do for him, poor old chap!"

"He might have chosen some other time to be ill," said Sally, who, not knowing the major, was inclined to be heartless.

"Well, yes. But we won't lose our holiday; we'll come again later, Sally."

H. Louisa Bedford

"We shan't! I'm perfectly certain we shan't!" cried Sally, turning away her head so that Paul should not see that there were tears in her eyes. "It was too delightful a plan to carry out."

The next day found Paul and his sister back in London. Sally was to go to an aunt for a few days, until Paul could settle his plans; and when he had seen her off from the station, he turned his own steps in the direction of the quiet square where his godfather had spent his solitary life since the days of his retirement from active service. His eyes turned instinctively to the windows, to see if the blinds were drawn down; but the house wore its usual aspect of dignified reserve, with its slightly opened casements. The imperturbable butler, who answered Paul's ring at the bell, seemed at first inclined to question his right to enter.

"My master is very sadly, sir; he's not fit to see any one."

"But he sent for me," said Paul, quietly. "Will you let him know, as soon as possible, that Paul Lessing has come in answer to his letter?"

At the mention of the familiar name Smith's manner altered perceptibly; he threw open the library door and ushered Paul in. It was scarcely a minute before he returned.

"My master is awake and will see you at once, sir."

"Has he been long ill?" Paul asked.

"It's been coming on gradual for a year or more, sir. Creeping paralysis is what the doctors call it. He's no use left in his legs, and very little in his arms or hands; but his brain seems as active as ever. He took a turn for the worse last week, and the end, they think, may come at any time."

"Thank you; I'll go upstairs now."

He entered the sick-room so quietly that the nurse, who sat by the bedside, did not hear him; but the grey head on the pillow turned quickly, and the dying eyes shone with eager welcome.

"I'm glad you've come; I thought you meant to leave it till too late," was the abrupt greeting.

"I was abroad, and did not get your letter at once," Paul said gently.

"And you came back? That's more than many fellows would have done. Nurse, draw up those blinds, and leave us, please; there are several things I have to say. No, you need not talk about my saving my strength. What good will it do? A few minutes more life, perhaps," he added testily, as he saw the nurse giving Paul some admonition under her breath. "Women are a nuisance, Paul; and at no time do they prove it more than when you are ill and under their thumb. There! take a seat close by me, where I can see you."

"You wanted to see me about something particular, your lawyer told me," said Paul, filled with pity at the sight of the perfectly helpless figure. "It may be that I can carry out some wish of yours. I should be glad to be of service to you."

Major Lessing did not answer for some minutes, and Paul ascribed his silence to exhaustion. In reality the keen eyes were scanning Paul's face critically, as if trying to read his character.

"I wanted to see you; and now you've come I don't know what to make of you. It has crossed my mind more than once since I've lain here, that I've been a rash fool to make a man I know so little of, my heir."

Paul could not repress an exclamation of astonishment; the news gave him anything but unmixed pleasure.

"It was surely very rash, sir. I've no possible claim upon you. I have scarcely even any connection with you except the name."

"That's it," said the major. "You have the name, and that must be carried on and a distant tie of relationship; and there's something else, Paul. Years ago I wanted to marry your mother. You are my godson; you might have been my real son, you see."

Paul felt a lump in his throat; this love-story of long ago was pathetic. His mother had died when he was still quite a child, but she lived in his memory as beautiful and fascinating.

"She was half Irish," he said.

The major nodded. "So, partly from sentimental reasons, and partly because there was no one better, I've left the property at Rudham to you," he went on with a smile. "There would have been plenty of money to have left with it; but I've made some very bad speculations lately, and lost a great deal. I took to speculation from sheer want of amusement. I was a good billiard player as long as I had the use of my limbs; but here I've been, literally tied by the legs, for the last two years. The only thing properly alive about me was my brain, and speculation has interested me; but I was badly hit ten days ago. There will be some money, but you won't be a rich man."

"I don't care about it," interposed Paul, eagerly.

"Then you ought to; a landlord poorly off is in a bad case in these days; and I want things kept as they are, Paul. I've not lived at Rudham, but I've kept my eye on it all the same; and what you call progress, and its attendant abominations, has not hurt it much yet. I made a mistake when I let the bishop nominate a successor to the living when old Gregg died three years ago. Curzon's a go-ahead fellow, from all that I hear; I don't want a go-ahead squire."

"I'm afraid you've made another mistake, and, if there's time, you had better undo it," said Paul, gravely.

"Do I look like a man who can re-arrange all his matters?" asked the Major, irritably. "After all, what I ask of you is no very hard thing to grant; simply to accept the good the gods provide, and let well alone."

"But that for me is an impossible condition," said Paul. "I cannot let things alone if I feel that I can better them. I'm in no way fitted for a country squire; I've been brought up on different lines from you, and arrived at very different conclusions. I am grateful to you for your thought of me, but I want to live my own life unfettered by any conditions."

"And this is how you show your readiness to carry out any wish of mine?" said the major, bitterly.

"I'm sorry; but I promised in the dark, not knowing that my principles would be involved."

"I'm glad to hear you have any. May I ask what you call yourself? A Lessing who is not a Conservative is not worthy of the name."

"I scarcely know what I am; but my friends call me a Socialist."

H. Louisa Bedford

"Then in Heaven's name, I've made a bigger blunder than the last!" said the squire, with an odd thrill in his voice.

"It's not my fault; and there may still be time to undo it," said Paul, rising, for the flush that crept to the major's temples warned him that the interview had been too long and too exciting. "I would thank you, if I could, for the thought of me, and I am sorry to have been the cause of disappointment, but it would not have been honest to hide my opinions."

"No; you've been honest enough, in all conscience. If there's yet time—" He broke off, turning away his head, and taking no notice of Paul's departure.

All that night Paul paced his room in deep thought. The scene he had witnessed had stirred him more than a little; and it grieved him to his heart that he had so seriously disturbed the last moments of a dying man.

"But I could not have hoodwinked him," he thought; "no honest man could. But to-morrow I'll prove to him that I am ready to help him in any way that I can. If he will only talk quietly, and keep his temper, he could surely suggest some more fitting heir than I; and the business details could be fairly quickly settled if I could take down his wishes and see his lawyer. He must yet have several days to live, I should think, with his extraordinary vitality of brain."

At a very early hour the following morning, therefore, Paul presented himself again at the house in the square, with the request that he might have a short interview with the major.

"Very sorry, sir," said Smith, with an added gloom of manner, "but my master's much worse; they don't think he'll live through the day. He was very restless last night; and nothing would satisfy him but that I should go off in the middle of the night and fetch Mr. Morgan—the lawyer as wrote to you, sir; but when I got him here my master had lost his power of speech. He knew Mr. Morgan quite well, but he could not make him understand what he wanted."

"And now?" asked Paul, pitifully.

"The doctor is just coming down the stairs, and will speak to you, sir."

Paul went out into the hall to meet him. "How did you find the major?" Paul inquired.

"Dead," replied the doctor, drawing on his gloves. "He died as I entered the room."

H. Louisa Bedford

CHAPTER III

FIRST IMPRESSIONS

"RUDHAM, Sunday Evening.

"DEAR SALLY,

"I did not, until now, believe myself a creature of impulse. That I am one is proved by the fact that, as I dropped my last letter to you into the post-box, I made up my mind to run down here and have a look round; and here I am. My surroundings I will describe later. I told you I had decided not to go to poor old Major Lessing's funeral for various reasons. I have a horror of humbug; and to pose as sole and chief mourner at the funeral of a man who had made me his heir by a fluke, and if he had lived an hour longer would have altered his will, seemed humbugging, to my mind. Also the funeral service, beautiful as it appears to those who can believe in it, means absolutely nothing to me; and I have scruples about appearing as if it did. Two surprises awaited me at Rudham: first, that by the same train by which I arrived Mrs. and Miss Webster got out upon the platform; and the beauty who fascinated you 'all of a heap' at Brussels, turns out to be the tenant of Rudham Court—*my* tenant, in fact!—a judgment upon me, you will say, for my unreasoning prejudice. Secondly, the extreme difficulty of getting a night's lodging, unless your character and circumstances are well known, was borne in forcibly upon my mind! An under-gardener of Mrs. Webster's took me up in the cart which carried your charmer's luggage.

"Judging by the size and number of the boxes, beauty needs a great deal of adorning, by the way! Then I was handed over to the village blacksmith, and, under the shelter of his name, I persuaded a Mrs. Macdonald to take me in. You would describe her as 'quite a darling!'"

"She and her husband are Scotch by birth, and still retain the soft intonation and pretty accent. They have no children—indeed, Mrs. Macdonald informs me that they have not long been married; and she must be fifty, and 'my John,' as she calls him, some ten years older; but I have never seen two people more in love with each other. If surroundings are an index to character they must be very nice people indeed. Let me try and describe my room, which is furnished with the solid simplicity of a hundred years ago. A grandfather clock ticks solemnly in the corner, two oak chairs stand on either side of the fireplace, with down cushions in print covers on the seats—a concession to modern luxury. In place of the cheap modern sideboard an open oak cupboard, whereon are displayed my dinner and tea-things, furnishes one side of the room, leaving just sufficient space for two Windsor chairs, polished to such a dangerous brightness that to sit upon them without sliding off requires more careful balance than to ride a bicycle. An oak table with twisted legs, and flaps that let up or down at will, is in the centre of the room. One almost expects clean rushes strewed upon the floor; instead there is linoleum of a neat design—black stars upon a white ground; and Mrs. Macdonald prides herself not a little upon the far-sighted policy that made her decide upon linoleum rather than carpet.

H. Louisa Bedford

"'It can be wiped over with a damp cloth every day, sir, and kept sweet and clean; and if you're feet are cold, I'm not saying that I'll mind your putting them on the rug, although I made it all myself'—which was kind of Mrs. Macdonald! My attention being thus drawn to the hearthrug, I discover that it's a work of art, in its way, knitted in with rags and tags of cloth, grave or gay in colouring, but harmonious in the general effect. You will think that I am developing a passion for detail, but it is rather that I wish to photograph exactly my first impressions of the place. There seems a primitive simplicity about it that must vanish at the first touch of modern progress like a pretty old fresco exposed to the light, and I feel myself like a traitor in the camp. If I decide to live here I shall probably be the motive force that will set the ball of progress rolling. Life here is almost stagnant, I fancy, unlike the river, which runs swift and strong along the side of the village. It separates from, rather than connects it with the outer world, for there are dangerous currents which make it not too safe for navigation; and to cross it you must either go to the ferry, half a mile off, or make for the bridge at Nowell four miles away. I found out all this by a stroll after tea, last evening, and a gossip with my new acquaintance, the blacksmith Allison. Gradually the talk turned to things parochial, and I discovered some characteristics of the go-ahead parson, whose appointment to the living my godfather gently deplored; and this was how it came about. A tall, powerful-looking man came swinging down the road at a brisk pace, nodding in quick, alert fashion to one and another as he passed, recognizing me as a stranger, but bidding Allison a cheerful good night as he passed on in the direction of the inn. By his dress I knew he must be the parson of the place. Allison, who had acknowledged his greeting only by a sideways nod, gave a grunt of assent when I asked him if it were so.

"'Curzon,' he said; 'that's his name, a meddlesome chap, if

ever there were one! Now the last rector were a real gentleman! You could please yourself about going to church or staying at home; but he were wonderful kind in sickness and such.'"

"And you miss the attention, I daresay?"

"'Well, I'm not saying that exactly. Mr. Curzon's wonderful took up with the sick folks and children, but it's us well ones he can't leave alone. His work's never done, as you may say. Now what do you suppose he's after to-night?' in a tone of angry argument."

"I really can't guess."

"'No; it's not likely you would. He makes believe as he's gone for a walk, but he'll be turning back again about such time as the men are turning out of the public there! Then, come next week, he'll be droppin' into one cottage or another about such time as the man comes in from work, and it'ull be, 'So and so, I'm afraid you had a glass too much on Saturday night. I wouldn't do it, if I was you;' and then he's sure to put in something about coming to church on Sunday."

"And do they?" I asked.

"'Some on 'em. Most of 'em, if I speaks the truth, gets tired of being told of it, I think, and goes just to pacify him, as you may, say; but I don't hold with it myself.'"

"Apparently this faithful shepherd does succeed in driving a very large proportion of his flock to church on Sunday. Allison and I are distinctly in a minority. I was nearly being carried there forcibly myself to-night; and I only escaped, I believe, because Mrs. Macdonald has evolved, from the label on my portmanteau that I am the coming squire, and must be

H. Louisa Bedford

allowed some liberty of opinion.

"'You'll be going to church to-night, sir,' she said, beginning the attack with gentle firmness. 'John and I lock up the house and hide the key under the mat, in case you come back before we do. We have a walk these summer evenings when church is over.'"

"Thank you, Mrs. Macdonald, you can leave the key in the door; I have writing to do."

"But you'll be going to church, for sure; you were not there this morning, I'm thinking, and the rector's sure to say something of him that's gone."

"I had not the courage of my opinions, like Allison. How could I grieve the kindly eyes that looked into mine? So I took refuge in weak evasion."

"'I've been over-worked and over-worried, Mrs. Macdonald, and my head aches, and I need rest and quiet.'"

"Well there, sir; you'll forgive my making so bold, but it will grieve the good man, if he knows you've come. And there's a-many will be disappointed not to catch a sight of you, besides."

"Whom do you mean by the good man?"

"There now! it slipped out without thinking. But it's what my John and I call Mr. Curzon, for we've never come across such a one as he."

"'And why am I to be a sort of show to the others?' I asked with some curiosity."

"'Ah! Because some of them begin to guess now who you are—not that John nor I are much given to talk. But when a neighbour asks your name, we couldn't keep it no longer—could we, sir?'"

"Certainly not. And they will all see me sooner or later, though it won't be at church to-night. I hope soon to know every one in the place."

"So finally I've been left in charge of the cottage, and have been writing ever since this long rigmarole to you. Mrs. Macdonald's words have given me food for reflection, and, the more I reflect, the more fully convinced I am how thoroughly unfitted I am to fill the place allotted to me. Had Major Lessing left me money enough to carry out my own wishes, I should have been inclined to put his property in the hands of a capable, fair agent, and do with it as Major Lessing suggested, and keep things very much as they are; but I find that I shall have little independent income apart from the property. To keep things in really working repair I shall probably have to raise the rents—which are absurdly low—which, of course, will be a very unpopular movement; and my being willing to live as simply as any of my tenants, will not in the least soften their feeling towards me. I shall not do anything in a hurry, but I shall first try and master my position. After so many years of a non-resident squire of a strictly conservative type, there must be need for improvements; but here again comes in the question of money. I am afraid that trip abroad must be put off for the present. How would it be for you to come here for a bit? I will sound Mrs. Macdonald on the subject to-morrow. If I undertake the management of things here myself, you would help me with accounts, etc., and I could take you on as my paid secretary! However this is looking too far ahead. I will keep this letter open and tell you the result of my advances to-morrow."

H. Louisa Bedford

"Monday Evening."

"I approached Mrs. Macdonald with much diplomacy this morning. She gave me the opening I sought by saying, when I ordered my dinner—

"I suppose you'll be leaving to-day or to-morrow, sir."

"On the contrary, you are making me so comfortable, that I was going to ask you to take me on for a few weeks, at any rate."

"But it isn't right or fitting that the likes of you should be living in a cottage such as this. The whole place belongs to you, I'm thinking."

"I suppose it does. But if I come to live here I shall start either in a cottage, or quite a small house, with a sister of mine who has no home, poor child! How she would like to join me here, by the way."

"Mrs. Macdonald played nervously with the string of her apron. I could see I had appealed to her motherly heart by representing you as a motherless orphan."

"'I suppose you haven't a second bedroom,' I suggested, following up my advantage."

"It's a slip of a thing; not fit for a lady, sir."

"After all, ladies are much the same as other women; and my sister might have the bigger bedroom and I the smaller."

"'There's my John,' doubtfully."

"Doesn't he like ladies?"

"'Not all of them, sir,' with a sudden burst of confidence. 'There's Mrs. Webster; she called here one day to know if I'd take in some of the washing—and he'd just come in from work,—and she marched into the kitchen and talked very loud. Though he's deaf he don't like no notice taken of it; and he told her it 'ud be time enough for me to work when he was laid by, and then he'd be sorry if I had to do it.'"

"'But, of course, if Macdonald does not like us we will leave at once,' I said, assuming that Mrs. Macdonald had agreed to have you. So you're to come, Sally; come as quickly as you can. Don't bring much luggage, for there is nowhere to put it; and pray remember to talk gently to our host. I cannot see why we should not double the size of this cottage—put in a bath-room, and get Mrs. Macdonald to do for us; but this will entirely depend upon your manners, you see. I was preparing to go out, when I saw a child's invalid carriage barring the entrance to the gate, and a child's clear voice was giving very impressive orders about the contents of a certain basket which was to be carried up to the door."

"You won't spill them, Nurse. You'll be sure not to spill them; they're so *very* ripe they'd burst if you did."

"No, darling; I'll carry them as carefully as new-laid eggs."

"The woman spoke like a lady; her tone was so gentle and refined."

"I was standing at the open door of the cottage, and went down the path to meet her, asking if I could take in the basket to Mrs. Macdonald."

"'But they are not for her; they're for you. But I'm afraid you're better and don't want them,' said the voice from the carriage outside."

H. Louisa Bedford

"'Whatever is inside that basket I'm sure to want,' I said, going out to my odd little visitor; 'but I don't quite know why you are so kind as to bring me things. I'm afraid there's some mistake; I shall be so disappointed if there is.'"

"The blue eyes that looked up into mine began to smile."

"'Shall you really? There can't be any mistake, because last night, as Nurse wheeled me out of church, I heard daddy talking to Mrs. Macdonald; and she said she'd got the new squire at home, but he'd a dreadful headache and couldn't come.'"

"I could scarcely help laughing; I certainly had not intended my words to be accepted so literally."

"'Who are you?' I asked, 'and what's in that basket? It wouldn't be manners to peep inside, would it?'"

"'Oh yes, it would,' with a delighted giggle. 'I'm Kitty—Kitty Curzon,—and daddy says it's my work to look after any one who is not well; and I'm to think what they will like, and take it to them. So, when I heard you had such a bad headache, I got Nurse to gather my last red gooseberries—they are *very, very* ripe,—and I've brought them for you; and can I have the basket, please?'"

"'Well, I can't accept them on the plea of headache: it's gone, you see; but perhaps you will be so kind as to leave them all the same, for if there is one thing I like more than another—'"

"'It's gooseberries,' interposed Kitty, eagerly; and I nodded assent."

"The child shot a triumphant glance at Nurse."

"'She said you would not want them, and I'd better ask daddy; but he likes me to think of things by myself. And then at the end of the day I tell him where I've been; and he'll be so surprised to-night, for he didn't know I'd heard about you.'"

"I carried off the basket, and brought it back, presently, empty."

"'I have not half thanked you, Kitty; but I am most grateful. How old are you, I wonder?'"

"There was a moment's hesitation. 'I'm not young at all; I'm nine, although you'd never think it, because I'm so small. Daddy says running about makes you grow, and I can't run.'"

"'Her back is not strong, sir,' said Nurse, hurriedly; and as I looked at the recumbent figure, I saw that the poor little child was deformed. It seemed a terrible pity, for the face and head are singularly pretty."

"That's why daddy says I must think of all the ill ones, because Nurse and he think so much about me."

"'Very well. I shall be sure and send for you directly there is anything the matter. I fancy you would do me more good than a doctor. And I've a sister coming, before long, and she will want companions. You will have to come to tea.'"

"Is she as old as I am?"

"A little older, I think."

"I'll come if daddy will let me; but Nurse must come too."

"By all means, and if you have any little brothers or sisters—"

"'I have not any. There's only me,' interposed Kitty, shaking her head."

"I wonder what her name is?"

"My sister's, do you mean? Sally. Rather a nice name, isn't it?"

"Evidently Kitty did not like it much, for she said she must be going; and went on her way, kissing her hand graciously, so I took off my hat and waved it."

"From Mrs. Macdonald I gather that my first visitor is Mr. Curzon's only child. He is a widower, it seems, and Kitty is the cause of his holding a country living. By my landlady's account he is simply wrapped up in her. I have been the round of the village to-day, making acquaintance with one and another as occasion offered. As I conjectured there seems plenty to be done; and it must be some months before I can stir hand or foot, before I can get things even into my own hands—not that the people here realize this in the very least. Indeed they are intellectually dead; they seem to possess no ambition of any sort."

"I went into the parish church on my way home. It is an interesting one, built about the end of the thirteenth century, with a magnificent tower that one can see for miles round. I found a great many monuments to the Lessings—a very virtuous lot, if their memorial tablets are to be trusted. The church has been carefully restored—quite recently, I fancy, by the look of it. Then I went into the churchyard, where a newly-filled-in grave showed me where my poor godfather had been laid. The sacristan, a very old, infirm man was putting it tidy; and to my astonishment I saw a low vase of white flowers placed in the very centre of the grave."

"'I suppose I am not mistaken,' I said. 'This must be Major Lessing's grave?'"

"Yes, sir."

"And who put the flowers?"

"'Miss Kitty, the little maid at the rectory. She said she'd thought he'd be lonely without any;' and the sacristan straightened his back with a little smile."

"'I hope you don't mind,' said a voice behind me. 'I've a notion your relative did not like flowers at a funeral, but I could not upset Kitty's conviction that he did.'"

"It was the rector who had come upon me unawares, and he did not pretend not to know me."

"'What can it matter now?' I answered. 'He'll know nothing of it.'"

"But I must stop, I've no time to describe the good man. Come and see him for yourself."

"Ever yours,

"PAUL LESSING."

CHAPTER IV

OPPOSING VIEWS

The man who some centuries earlier had built Rudham Court, had been wiser than the generation in which he lived in his choice of a site. Instead of a valley he had chosen the side of a hill, and the sloping foreground had been levelled into a succession of terraces, giving the impression of an almost mountainous ascent to the house from the road which lay beneath. The house, not beautiful in itself, was softened by the hand of time into a dull red that contrasted harmoniously with the group of trees behind it, and the gravelled terrace in front with its box-bordered beds was a blaze of colour in the brilliant sunshine of the August morning. It was bordered by a low stone wall along which two peacocks strutted with almost ridiculous self-consciousness of their beauty. In the very centre was a flight of steps which descended to the bowling-green beneath, where the yew hedge which grew round it had been fantastically cut into the shape of an embattlemented parapet, framing the distant view into a series of charming little pictures: here a glimpse of the river, there a delightful vignette of the church.

Across the velvety turf of the green tripped Rose Lancaster, dangling a basket from her arm, a picture herself in her pink cambric frock and befrilled apron, a little French cap set upon her head which enhanced the beauty of the golden hair. Her skin was of the delicate colouring that so often accompanies fair hair, the mouth generally wore a smile displaying Rose's pretty dimples, and the great blue eyes were half concealed by the long lashes. She made her way to the wicket-gate at the far end of the green, to a winding path through a wood which led to the rose-garden below, and gave a start of pretended surprise when Tom Burney broke off from his task of mowing the grass paths which separated the beds, with an exclamation of delight.

"You here!" said Rose, who had watched the direction of his steps from a window above. "I've come after some roses, if I can find any. Nothing satisfies Miss Webster but roses on the mantel-shelf of her sitting-room, and it does not matter to her whether they are in season or out. Roses she must have. Are there any coming on, Tom?"

"Bother the roses!" said Tom, impatiently. "You've been back nearly a fortnight, and have not spoken a word to me yet."

"That's ungrateful. I walked to church with you on Sunday evening, and I told you lots of things I did when we were away."

"Dixon joined us, and you let him!" said Tom, angrily.

"How could I help it?" Rose answered, arching her pretty brows. "I could not say I didn't want him, could I?"

"Are you going to walk with him or me, Rose? I asked you before you went away, and I want to know now."

Rose meditatively clipped off a bud, crying out a little as a thorn pricked her finger, holding out the injured member for

H. Louisa Bedford

Tom to look at; but he looked over it at her, a flush on his handsome face.

"It may be play to you; it isn't to me," he said, his voice shaking a little. "Did you get the letter I wrote?"

"I don't know; I forget. I had a lot of letters. Yes, I expect I did."

"And you didn't trouble to answer it?"

"It's clear you don't know what a lot a lady's maid has to do when she's travelling," said Rose, petulantly. "It's 'Lancaster' here and 'Lancaster' there, and you've no sooner packed up than you begin unpacking again. What time should I get for answering letters?'"

"I wanted to know if you'd thought over what I said?"

"You can't expect me to remember what you said six weeks ago."

"You do remember, only you don't want to give a straight answer. That's about it," said Tom, bitterly.

"I like walking with you both, though not together. There!" cried Rose, with a defiant toss of her head. "I'm young; I don't mean to be tied!"

"But you'll care for the one who loves you best, and that's me!" burst out poor Tom. "Dixon may be smarter, and he's a deal better off; but he's a glib sneak, and I know it. I'll wait three months, and then I'll have my answer; and if it's 'No' I'll be fit to drown myself," and Tom's voice broke off in something very like a sob.

Rose was flattered but frightened at realizing her power over the lad. It was like a book, that he should threaten to drown himself for love of her; but of course he did not mean it. She was sorry for him; when she was with him she almost believed she loved him, but at any rate she need not decide now. Three months hence she might know her own mind.

"Well, we'll wait three months and see what happens; and meantime I do hope you'll be careful not to quarrel with Dixon."

"I shall if he comes in my way," declared Tom, sturdily. "I don't wonder he wants you himself—any man would; but he should play fair."

"He's no quarrel with you; he said you were a decent sort of a lad, the other day."

Tom clenched his fist involuntarily. "That's just it!—he's always trying to run me down in your eyes. A lad, indeed! I'm a man who wants the same girl he does, and that's yourself, Rose."

Rose laughed gaily; it was nice to find herself so much in request.

"Man or boy, I can't stay talking to you all day. Pick me any roses there are, and let me go. I believe" (in a lowered undertone) "that I hear the ladies talking up there on the bowling-green. They've come out to sit in the shade, I expect."

Rose's conjecture was right, for, as she went back to the house, she caught a glimpse of Miss Webster and her mother seated under the large tree at the far end of the lawn.

"How pretty she is," said May Webster, following her retreating figure with lazy eyes. "As pretty as the roses she carries. I do hope she won't get snapped up at once. She is a pleasant little thing to have about one—which reminds me, mother. I saw a pretty girl of a different type in the village yesterday, whom I believe to be Miss Lessing. What are you going to do about her and her brother?"

"Nothing at present, I think. One really can't leave cards on a cottage!"

"But you might on the people in it. We can't very well ignore the squire of the place who is also our landlord."

"It will be time enough to recognize him when he behaves like other people."

"I don't see that he's a bit more peculiar than the University men who take to slumming. Anybody may do anything nowadays," May said with a little laugh.

"He doesn't even come to church," persisted Mrs. Webster.

"A weakness shared by many men."

"But his sister might and *ought*," replied her mother, severely.

"Mr. Curzon seems to think it equally necessary for men and women," said May, mischievously.

"Oh yes. Of course he's a dear good man, and I wish we were all like him, but we aren't," answered Mrs. Webster, resigning all hope of anything but moral mediocrity with a gentle sigh. "He says Mr. Lessing is a very nice fellow; but you can't quite rely on his opinion: he's a good word for every one."

"Which is delightful, but not amusing; and one does need amusement, mother. Suppose we call at the cottage and follow up the call by an invitation to dinner. We might ask the rector to meet them."

"The worst of asking the rector is that he always wants something," said Mrs. Webster, a little plaintively.

"That we haven't got?"

"Oh, May, you know quite well what I mean! It must be the heat that is making you so argumentative. Mr. Curzon always has some pet hobby on hand for which he wants money, and of course he ought to have it; but really, just now, what with a trip abroad, and the London house to paint and paper throughout, I've not so much in hand as usual."

"Enough for the rector's last hobby, I dare say. At any rate let's risk it. If we all air our different views we might have an exciting evening."

"I wish things were as they used to be. The old major was such a thorough gentleman. It was quite a pleasure to give him a bed or dinner when he came down."

"Is not this man a gentleman, then?"

"Oh, my dear, I hope so; but he has queer views, if all I hear be true. I'm sure, if he says anything at dinner about our being all equal, I shan't be able to hold my tongue. We never were and never can be."

"I believe Mr. Curzon thinks we are; only he likes poor people *much* the best. He says the truest gentleman he ever

H. Louisa Bedford

came across is old Macdonald."

"Now it is wild talk like that that makes me sometimes distrust Mr. Curzon; and he ought to know better, being of such good family himself," said Mrs. Webster, fretfully. "Is it not at the Macdonalds that the Lessings are lodging? As you seem to wish it, we will call this afternoon."

Paul Lessing was out when the smart carriage and pair drew up at the Macdonald's cottage in the course of the afternoon; and Sally had to receive her two visitors alone. Mrs. Webster's ample presence seemed to fill the tiny sitting-room; but she placed herself graciously enough in one of the cushioned elbow-chairs, whilst May subsided into the slippery Windsor as gracefully as if it were the softest sofa. There was something about Sally that pleased her; it may have been a certain originality and freshness of manner, or the unconscious admiration that shone in the dark eyes. Nothing in its way pleases a handsome woman more than the admiration of her own sex. Be this as it may, May Webster laid herself out to charm, and did it very successfully, and by judicious management prevented her mother from asking any leading questions as to Mr. Lessing's future line of conduct. Mrs. Webster's small talk so often took the line of asking questions.

Paul was not properly grateful when he found the cards upon the mantelshelf.

"It's a dreadful bore; but I'm afraid it can't be helped. You can return the call sometime, and there will be an end of it."

"There may be for you, but there won't be for me!" said Sally, with some spirit. "I'm catholic in my choice of comp-anions, and mean to include everybody who cares to know me. Mrs. Macdonald is charming, and Allison amuses me, and Mrs. Pink and I have made friends over the baby; but why I should refuse a proffer of friendship from Miss Webster, because she happens to be a beauty and dresses well, I don't exactly see!"

"Friendship!" echoed Paul, scornfully. "How little you know of smart people and their ways. Friendship with them means a stepping-stone to higher things; your means and your position must give them a leg up in the world. Now we have neither."

"You are shaking my faith in you, Paul. You are judging without knowing."

"I am not judging the Websters individually—only the class to which they belong; of which I *do* know something, and you nothing."

"Well, I think I will learn for myself then!" cried Sally. "I'll start by believing people as nice as they appear, until I find them otherwise."

"And are Mrs. and Miss Webster 'nice,' as you call it?" asked Paul, his curiosity overcoming his vexation.

"I did not like Mrs. Webster much: the room did not seem big enough to hold her."

"I told you so!" said Paul, triumphantly.

"Oh, Paul! you might be a woman," replied Sally, with mocking laughter. "But listen; Miss Webster is as nice as she looks! Can you want more?"

"It's a good thing to be young and enthusiastic."

"Certainly better than being old and cynical," retorted Sally, saucily.

The next morning's post brought a crested envelope, directed in a dashing hand, to Sally, inviting Paul and herself to dinner at the Court on the following evening.

"We shall be simply a family party," wrote the lady; "but, with such near neighbours, I thought it more friendly to invite you for the first time quite informally."

"You don't want to go!" exclaimed Paul, who felt the meshes of the society net closing round him.

"Of course I do. I want to see your house, and to feel what it would be like to live there."

"I don't believe you have a proper frock to go in. A coat and skirt won't do."

"What nonsense! I've an evening dress, of a sort; and they don't invite my frock, but me!"

"We'll go, then, as you've set your heart upon it; but I feel as if it were the letting out of water."

Certainly Paul had no reason to complain of Sally's appearance when she came down ready dressed for her dinner on the following evening. In her simple white dress, cut away at the throat, with a soft muslin fichu tied in front with long ends falling to the bottom other skirt, she looked, as old Macdonald afterwards remarked to his wife, "as a lady should:" fair, and fresh, and young. Her dusky hair waved prettily upon her forehead, and half concealed her ears; the face it framed was not, strictly speaking, pretty, but it was bright and animated, and the dark eyes and eyebrows were handsome.

"I've won one person's approval at any rate," said Sally, merrily, as they started on their way. "I went in to bid Macdonald good night, and Mrs. Macdonald said, as she helped me on with my cape, that 'my John' likes ladies to wear white dresses and have pale faces. He could not abide colour, except in flowers."

"Then you are fulfilling your mission, Sally, and winning your way into Macdonald's good graces. We shan't be turned out."

"It's my first dinner-party, Paul. Do you realise the importance of the occasion? I've had no coming-out like other girls."

"That's why you are so much jollier than most of them," said Paul, betrayed into a compliment.

From the moment they entered the drive-gate, and began the ascent to the house, Sally looked about her with eager interest, breaking into exclamations of delight as each step revealed some fresh beauty to her eyes.

"It's a dangerous experiment to have brought you. You will be horribly discontented with Macdonald's, after this."

"I shan't. But if this place were mine, I should live here, and make it a joy to everybody about me. I would not want to keep it to myself," Sally said—

But the front door was reached, and a footman was at hand to help her off with her cloak; and in another instant the door of the long drawing-room was thrown wide, and Sally, with the un-self-consciousness of simplicity, heard herself announced, and found her hand in Mrs. Webster's, who retained it as she led her on towards a tall, handsome man who stood talking to Miss Webster.

"Mr. Curzon, allow me to introduce Miss Lessing. You've been away with your little Kitty, so I don't think you've met each other yet."

Then Sally realized that she stood face to face with the good man, and that he was to take her in to dinner, so that she would have time to consider him carefully. Mrs. Webster placed her hand graciously on Paul's arm when dinner was announced, and May trailing yards of amber-coloured silk behind her, sailed in by herself.

The dinner-table was oval, and Sally found herself seated between the Rector and May; on the other side sat Paul, with Mrs. Webster and May to talk to alternately. The very perfection of her surroundings engaged Sally's attention at first: the delicately shaded lights shining down on the dainty flowers, and silver and glass; the dinner, remarkable rather for elegance than profusion; the family portraits on the wall, bewigged and befrilled, which stood at ease, and glanced down on the company with a sort of haughty indifference; the heavy, handsome furniture combining beauty with comfort; and last, but not least, May herself, whose beauty in her evening dress was simply dazzling.

Paul, reduced to commonplaces, was asking Mrs. Webster if the place suited her.

"A leading question, Mr. Lessing," she answered, with a sort of heavy playfulness. "I've no doubt you would be glad to hear it did not. But we are so fond of it, May and I; it's just the country place we want for the summer months. We are always in London for the season. But our lease is nearly run out, you know; and then, I'm afraid, naughty man! you will not let us renew it."

"Why not? I'm not likely to get better tenants," said Paul, politely.

"But you may be wanting to live here yourself, you see."

"Such a plan is very far from my thoughts at present. I neither wish, nor can afford it."

"But where else *can* you go?" asked Mrs. Webster, as if her life depended on the answer.

The plea of poverty must be ignored; it was only advanced because Mr. Lessing was her landlord!

"I've not decided yet. Sally and I are quite happy where we are."

"But you could not go on like that. It hardly seems right, you know."

"I don't see where the wrong comes in."

"Your very position as squire; you will be expected to be an employer of labour, you see."

"So I suppose I shall be, in time, although perhaps not about my house and garden. There are a great many things that will have to be done in the place when I get my affairs into order."

"Ah yes, of course; it's wonderful how the money flies. Here's Mr. Curzon insisting that the schools must be enlarged; I expect you are like him, and think that everybody ought to know everything, and that each child must have so many cubic feet! I'm sure I can't cope with it all. I only know we, who are a little better off, have to pay for it. He wants

H. Louisa Bedford

me to give a hundred pounds, and I tell him I really can't: fifty is the utmost, and that is more than I can afford. I advise you to keep clear of him to-night; he's sure to ask you to subscribe a similar sum."

"It's a voluntary school, I suppose?" said Paul, glancing across at the rector. "I could not subscribe to that; I'm in favour of a board school, you see."

Sally, looking from one to the other scented trouble, for Mr. Curzon broke off in the middle of a sentence, and his smiling, kindly face grew grave as he gazed steadily back at her brother. There was a moment of uncomfortable silence.

"I was going to call and discuss the matter of the school with you," said Mr. Curzon, at last; "but I did not mean to introduce the subject to-night."

"Of course not. We could not possibly allow it; could we, mother?" interposed May, with an air of relief. "I feel at the present moment we all need more cubic feet. It's so very hot; I almost think we could sit outside." And as she spoke a general move was made for the terrace, where seats and tables were arranged.

As neither of the men took wine they did not stay behind; and May, who was clever enough to see that they were both ready to show fight for their individual opinions, engaged Paul in conversation, whilst Mr. Curzon carried off Sally to see the bowling-green by moonlight.

"I never saw anything so quaintly pretty," Sally said. "The yew hedge with its succession of views suits it exactly."

"Yes, doesn't it?" replied her companion. "This is naturally my favourite;" and he paused at the opening where, below, the church stood out grand and stately against the evening sky. "Is it not a grand old tower? It stands just as a church should; it dominates the place."

The ring of enthusiasm in his voice brought an answering thrill into Sally's heart.

"Are you sure that it does really?" she asked, moved by a sudden impulse.

"I hope so; I pray God it may be so. If not in my time then in another's."

CHAPTER V

A QUESTION OF EDUCATION

"I can't think why you, or any reasonable man, should object to a board school?" said Paul, who had been expounding his views at some length to the rector. "The people should have a voice in the matter of their children's education; and it can't be fair that any particular system of religion should be forced upon them. In a place like this you would be pretty certain to come out at the head of the poll, and, if religious teaching seems such an essential, you would be allowed to give it with limitations."

"With limitations that would practically make it useless," said Mr. Curzon. "I am prepared to make any sacrifice rather than surrender the religious training of the children God has given to my care. It will be a hard matter, with you against me, but I must stick fast by my principle."

"In a few more years there won't be a voluntary school left in the country," said Paul.

"Mine shall be one of the last to die," replied Mr. Curzon.

"You are fully persuaded that you are carrying out the wishes of your people."

"I am sure that, as far as I know it, I shall be doing my duty by them—and that must come first; but they shall have an opportunity of expressing their opinion. I am going to call a meeting about the enlarging of the school, and I shall try and persuade every one to attend it."

"Including myself?" inquired Paul, with a rather sceptical smile.

"I shall wish you, of course, to be there."

"But I can only be there in opposition to your views," Paul said.

"A clergyman gets used to opposition," replied Mr. Curzon, quietly; "but if the school is to be continued under the management of myself and my churchwardens, it shall be no hole-and-corner business: it shall be with the consent and confidence of the majority of my people."

Paul rose to go; and there was rather a troubled look on his face as he took Mr. Curzon's out-stretched hand. It was such a kindly, friendly grip.

"I'm afraid we cannot help coming across each other as we both have the courage of our opinions; but at least you will believe that I have the social development of the village very near at heart."

"And there, at least, we agree," said Mr. Curzon, smiling; "but with me their spiritual welfare is even more urgent."

Kitty's little carriage was drawn up at the door, as she was just returning from an outing. She greeted Paul with a beaming face, which, as he came closer, grew clouded with anxiety.

H. Louisa Bedford

"I'm afraid you've got another headache, and I've got nothing to bring now," she said. "Blackberries wouldn't do. They are rather nasty, daddy thinks."

"I've not got a headache, Kitty, thank you," said Paul, leaving the question of blackberries in abeyance. "What made you think I had?"

"You were frowning; but perhaps it was the sun in your eyes. Has your sister bigger than me come yet?"

"Oh yes; she has been here quite a time, and you have not been to see her."

"I've been away; did not you know?—away with daddy," with a proud glance up at her father. "It was lovely; he had no one to think of but me, and I was with him on the beach nearly all day long."

"Ah, that's how you come to have such roses in your cheeks. Well, when are you coming to have tea with Sally and me? You shall choose your own day."

"Would to-morrow do? It's Sunday; and daddy likes me to have all the happiest things on Sunday. But I forgot; Nurse was to come, too, but she goes out on Sunday afternoon."

The sweet-faced woman who wheeled Kitty about gave an amused little laugh.

"It would be rather nice for you to go this once alone, Miss Kitty; and I could wheel you there on my way out—"

"And Sally and I could bring you home. Would not that do?" said Paul to Mr. Curzon.

"If you are sure you will not be troubled with her."

"Oh dear, no; it has been a long-standing engagement—has it not, Kitty?"

"Daddy dear, lift me out, please!" said Kitty, when Paul had gone on his way. "I like him so much, although I don't remember his name. It's rather a funny one, but I like him; he has such kind eyes."

Mr. Curzon tenderly lifted his little daughter out of her carriage, but made no answer to her remark about their new neighbour. To himself he was free to admit that the new squire's views troubled him sorely.

"We are to have our first tea-party to-morrow, Sally. I have invited the district visitor."

"Who?" asked Sally, in considerable astonishment.

"Kitty Curzon—whose loving care for my head has won my heart. The child persists in believing that I live in a chronic state of headache, and resorts to her own methods of cure. Ours is a friendship doomed to be nipped in the bud, alas! Let us make the most of it while it lasts."

"What is to kill it?"

"The father is the difficulty; he has caught sight of my cloven hoof this morning, and, depend upon it, he will not trust Kitty to us often. He had to consent to her coming this morning, for she arranged it all under his very eyes; and I saw he had not the heart to thwart her. She's a young woman who evidently gets her own way up to a certain point; but unless I'm greatly mistaken, the fatherly fiat will go forth that the less she sees of us the better."

H. Louisa Bedford

"I would rather she did not come at all, then," said Sally, hotly.

"I wouldn't; she has chosen this tea as her Sunday treat," Paul answered with a humorous smile.

By four o'clock on the morrow the little invalid carriage stopped at the Macdonald's gate, and Paul ran down to greet his visitor.

"Wait a moment, Kitty; Nurse and I between us can lift the whole thing in, and then she can go on for her outing, and you shall be left to Sally and me."

Kitty's eyes looked beyond Paul at Sally, who stood smiling behind.

"You did not tell me she was grown-up like everybody else," she answered irrelevantly.

"Oh, there's a lot of difference even between grown-up people, as I will presently show you," said Paul. "Meanwhile, before you talk to Sally, we'll get you into the cottage."

"Shall you carry me, like daddy? I can walk on crutches, but it hurts me rather," said Kitty. And Paul lifted her in his strong arms as gently as if she were a baby, and Sally followed with the crutches, her soul filled with pity for the child so perfectly developed as far as the waist, but whose legs were twisted and helpless.

Evidently poor Kitty had some affection of the spine. Sally felt her pity almost misplaced before the afternoon was over; Kitty's enjoyment of life in general, and her present entertainment in particular was so genuine, and her laughter so infectious.

By a happy inspiration Mrs. Macdonald had suggested that the tea should be held in the orchard behind the house, and Kitty's carriage was placed under the tree which bore the rosiest apples, one or two of which fell with a flop at her feet.

"Such as comes to little missy she must take home with her," said Macdonald, smiling benignantly from his seat in the kitchen, and bestowing a meaning glance at Paul, who, mindful of the hint, shook the boughs as he handed Kitty her tea, bringing a shower of red fruit about her.

The conversation never flagged; Kitty's life seemed full of interest, both at home and abroad, and she was fast friends, apparently, with every soul in the place, including Allison, who had won her affection for ever by presenting her with a Persian kitten, whom she brought down regularly once a week to call upon its former owner. When the bells began to chime for evening service Kitty signified her wish to depart.

"We could take little missy," said Macdonald. "We'll be going that way ourselves."

"No, thank you," said Paul. "We promised to take you home —did not we, Kitty?"

Had he realized quite what the fulfilment of that promise involved, he might have been inclined to accept the Macdonald's offer, for when he and Sally had wheeled their visitor as far as the rectory, and were going to enter, she shook her head vigorously.

"We can't get in there—it will be all locked up—every one's gone to church. Please take me on! my carriage goes into the

H. Louisa Bedford

belfry, and, as I lie there, I can see all down the church."

There was no disobeying such clear directions, so Paul, with a smile, humbly did as he was bid.

"Is that all you want?" he asked, when he had adjusted Kitty's carriage to the exact angle which she liked best.

He was in a hurry to slip out before the service began; Sally waited for him outside.

"Oh no; I haven't got my book and things," said Kitty. "They are in the box in the corner; daddy had it made for me, and here's the key," producing a key on a string from round her neck. "There's a nice red one you can use that belongs to Nurse."

By the time Paul had unlocked the box and found the books, Kitty's hands were devoutly folded in prayer, and her eyes fast shut. She opened them presently with a bright smile.

"Thank you," she half-whispered. "Now if you bring that chair close to me, you'll find my places for me; Nurse always does. I've not learned to read so very long—daddy would not let me."

Paul, feeling himself a victim of circumstance, fetched the chair and seated himself.

"I suppose he's forgotten to say his prayers," thought Kitty, as she noticed that he neither knelt down nor even placed his hand over his eyes, which were the varying methods of paying homage to God, that she had observed the men of the congregation adopted when they came into church.

Paul found his position a singular one. He had not been

present at a service of any description since his college days. It would not be true to say that he had lost his belief; he had never had any. He might well question the necessity of religious education, for he had had none himself. He and Sally had been baptized as babies, just because their mother had wished it; but after her death their father, who cared for none of these things, left their religious training to chance.

"Speak the truth, and behave like a gentleman," he said to Paul, when he was sent at an early age to school; "and if ever you get into a scrape, come to me and tell me all about it."

It was a very simple moral code, and Paul lived by it both at school and college; and before his college course was ended his father had died. Christianity had not appealed to him in any way; he regarded it as a worn-out system of religious belief that had been a moral force in the world, but was dying now, slowly perhaps, but surely. Perhaps in a remote village like this, where a Rector of strong personality was at the head of affairs, it might be fanned into a flame for a time, but it would not last. It certainly had a semblance of life to-night, Paul admitted, as the congregation rose to its feet at the opening bars of the voluntary, and the white-robed choir entered, followed by Mr. Curzon. There was scarcely an empty seat, and there were as many men present as women; and they were there, apparently, not to look on but to worship, if hearty singing or burst of response were any criterion. There was a scarcely a voice silent save Paul's own.

Viewed as a picture it was a pretty one, framed as it was by the high narrow Early English arch which opened from the belfry into the nave. First came the bowed heads of the kneeling people, and, through the beautiful old screen which separated chancel from nave, the altar shone out in strong relief against its background of soft-coloured mosaic, the rays of the western sun giving an added touch of brilliance to its decoration of cross and flowers.

But Kitty's hand was laid upon Paul's arm, and "Psalms, please!" brought him back from his reverie to his duty. He did not keep her waiting again, and he was interested by watching the sensitive, eager little face. There was no question that the child was following the service heart and soul; but when the sermon time came she was fairly tired out, and, turning her head a little on one side, she was soon fast asleep.

"If the Lord be God, follow Him," said Mr. Curzon; and Paul glanced up at the preacher, and noticed that every head was turned in the same direction. And yet it was no great eloquence that held them, but a certain manly simplicity of speech which carried conviction of the preacher's absolute sincerity. He prefaced his sermon with a notice of a public meeting that was to be held about the schools in the course of the coming week, at which he begged the attendance of all interested in the subject of education. The time had come when the schools must be enlarged, and he put the question of whether this should be done by private subscription, or by turning the school into a board school, very simply before his people, telling them that a grave question was involved in the decision—that of religious education.

"There are those among you who will say that in this matter the parsons want it all their own way; but, for myself, I emphatically deny the charge. I want God's way, and it is not until after much thought and prayer that I venture to place this matter before you to-night. It is one that I, as shepherd of this flock, must talk to you about, for holy hands have been laid upon my head, and the souls of all in this place are committed solemnly to my charge; and I must claim the little ones for the Master whom I serve, I wish to retain the right to train them as faithful and true members of Christ and His Church. I should not be faithful to my office unless I try to make you fully grasp the danger I believe to lurk in education that is robbed of its crowning glory—the knowledge of God."

Paul listened to the simple appeal which followed with interest not unmixed with irritation.

"He has the whip-hand over me; he rules his people by their hearts rather than by their heads," he said to Sally, afterwards, when he was giving her the gist of the sermon. "Parsons have a greater chance of propagating their views than any other set of men. Twice a day every Sunday they can lay down the law with never a soul to gainsay them."

"But lots of us don't go to listen," said Sally.

Paul laughed. "Well, no; I don't think there are many country congregations like the one I saw to-night. I'm not sorry to have been there for once. In future we'll fix some other day than Sunday for our visitor. I really could not hurt the child's feelings, and yet I cannot be led along a victim at her chariot wheels."

"I can't think why you take so much notice of her? You've never cared for a child before."

"She bought me with ripe gooseberries," Paul answered laughing. "I couldn't refuse a child's friendship any more than a dog's."

The Rector's sermon was fully discussed at the forge the following evening.

"Says I to Mr. Lessing to-day when we was talking together

about this eddication business, 'It's all very well sayin' as we must make the schools so fine and grand, but what I wants to know is, who's goin' to pay?" said Allison. "Them as has got the money, I s'pose."

"What did he say?" asked Tom Burney.

"'If I have my way it'll be thrown upon the rates.' But I'm not sure I'm with him there. Once let the rates run up, and we dunno where we are. Seems to me, with all his free-and-easy ways, and his living like one of us, he's a bit close-fisted— not a bit like the old major. Depend upon it, he don't want to put down his cool hundred; and that's why he talks so brisk about the rates. There's something about it as I've not got clear yet, for the rector comes along this morning, quite cheery like, and sings out as he passes, 'Comin' to the school meetin' a Friday, Allison? Room for all. I wants this school business settled.'"

"We couldn't settle it no better than it is at present, I'm thinking," interposed Macdonald gently. "To hear the rector talk a Sunday night about it were grand, that it was; and, if it's money he wants, there isn't one of us that oughtn't to help him."

"Rich fellers like you can talk about money!" retorted Allison, with withering scorn; "but for me, who makes every penny I earns, he may think hisself well off to get the five shillin's I gives him every year for those blessed schools. I'll stick to that five, neither more nor less, unless the squire gets his way; and then I won't give nothink but what I'm made to." But Allison found himself without an audience. With the mention of money the company had dispersed.

CHAPTER VI

A VOTE OF CONFIDENCE

"It must take it out of one dreadfully to be so terribly in earnest," said May Webster, softly stroking the pug dog that lay curled up in her lap.

"As who?" asked her mother, looking up from her writing.

"As Mr. Curzon; you might think his life depended on this school business. I really could not follow all he said this afternoon; but, apparently, he and Mr. Lessing have come to grief already about it. There's another earnest one—with this difference between them: that Mr. Curzon is earnest and agreeable, and Mr. Lessing earnest and disagreeable."

"He's more tiresome than disagreeable, May. I call it tiresome to live in a cottage instead of a house, and to keep his sister from church—I suppose that that is his doing,—and to upset us all when we are quiet and happy. He's paying such high wages, they say, to the men he has set at work over the drainage of some of his cottages, that I expect all our men will be asking us to raise theirs."

"I wonder which of them is right?" said May, returning to the subject of the schools.

"Mr. Curzon, of course; he's a clergyman, my dear!"

"Then you will go to the meeting to-night."

"You must be crazed, May, to think of such a thing. I go to a school meeting! If there is one type of woman I dislike more than another, it's the one to be found on platforms."

"I had not thought of you on a platform exactly. It only occurred to me that you would give Mr. Curzon your moral support, as your sympathies go with him. You carry weight, you see," which was true in more senses than one.

Mrs. Webster put the most favourable interpretation upon the phrase.

"Of course, if you really think it my duty, May," she said, softening visibly, "and would come with me—"

"Oh, I intend going anyhow," interposed May, carelessly.

"It's such a new departure for you to take a prominent part in parish things," exclaimed Mrs. Webster.

"Oh, parish has nothing to do with it! I'm going as a disinterested spectator to see the two earnest ones fight it out."

"My dear!" remonstrated her mother in a shocked tone.

"If I have a bias it's in favour of the rector. I don't pretend to understand the merits of voluntary versus board schools; but, as you say, a clergyman is always right—most probably Mr. Curzon's is the better cause, and most certainly he is the better man."

"Dear, dear; and we shall have to dine at seven, and keep as we are, I suppose?" with a glance at the stately folds of her brocade dress.

"Yes; we won't treat a school meeting like a theatre," said May, laughing. "Will it be considered unduly flippant on my part to go in this muslin? or ought I to wear black, as at a funeral?"

"It cannot signify in the least; a change of dress would not alter your flippant mind," replied her mother, with unusual smartness. "Dear Mr. Curzon has really convinced me that it is a most important subject, so I don't mind making a sacrifice for once in a way."

"By dining an hour earlier than usual and not changing your dress! All right, mother; I'll order the carriage for ten minutes to eight. We may as well be punctual."

The back benches of the schoolroom were crowded to overflowing when May and her mother entered that evening.

"It's very hot, May. I'm not sure that I can stay," said Mrs. Webster, pausing in the doorway.

"Oh yes, mother; we'll see it through to the bitter end," said May, in an undertone. "There are seats in the front."

Mrs. Webster picked her way daintily through the crowd, and Mr. Lessing, who was seated at the end of one of the desks, stood up to let her pass. May's skirt caught against a nail, as she followed, and Paul bent to set it free; but as May turned smiling to thank him, it gave her a faint shock of surprise to read the dislike that found expression in his eyes. Her smile faded, and she passed on her way with a haughty little bow.

"I wonder why he hates me? I am not aware that any man has ever viewed me with honest dislike before," she thought, as she took her seat by her mother.

Paul, on his side, was inspired with the same unwilling admiration and active irritation as on the occasion of their first meeting at Brussels. Beautiful she undoubtedly was; so beautiful that his eyes unconsciously followed her every movement. The cordial greeting she accorded the rector—so different from her bow to himself,—and the poise of her head, as she turned to look at the rows of expectant faces behind her, giving a smiling nod to Mrs. Macdonald, who, duly impressed with the gravity of the occasion, sat by the side of her John with her hands clasping a clean pocket-handkerchief as if she were at church. Paul tried to define the cause of his annoyance as he looked at her.

"It is the hard crust of indifference which society people cultivate to such perfection; it's the assurance which beauty assumes. She has come here most probably in search of a new sensation," he thought.

But the rector, who sat on a platform at the end of the room, with his two churchwardens, was already on his feet, and Paul pocketed his annoyance and settled himself to listen.

"My friends," he began, "we have met to-night to consider on what basis our school shall be carried on; whether at this crisis in school affairs, which demands an outlay of some seven or eight hundred pounds, the voluntary system shall be continued; or whether it shall be turned into a board school, paid for out of the rates, and managed by a committee chosen by the votes of the people. It is not a question that it has been necessary for us to discuss before. My people, I believe to a man, have been content to entrust the education of their children, the practical management of the school, to the churchwardens and myself, supporting us by their voluntary subscriptions; but a murmur has reached our ears that some of you are dissatisfied with this arrangement. My churchwardens and I feel reluctant to retain the management of the school unless fully assured that we are fulfilling the wishes of the majority of the people. You one and all know my views on this subject, and the principle that I believe to be involved in your decision. Whichever scheme is followed will mean a considerable outlay of money. It is for you to decide whether that money shall be exacted from you by rate, or whether it shall be given freely and liberally out of the means with which God has blessed you."

The rector closed with a request that any one wishing to address the meeting would come up to the platform, and, in answer to the challenge, Paul Lessing walked up the room and took his stand before the people. He was clever, and gifted with readiness of speech, but something in the audience baffled him; whether it was the stolid imperturbability of the faces in the back benches, or May Webster's half-amused, half-scornful smile just below him, he could not decide. But he pulled himself together, determining to state his case as shortly and clearly as he could.

He expressed no doubt that in times past the school had been well and ably managed; but he reminded them that Government had seen fit to place in their hands a power which the people in country places were slow to recognize: that of exercising a control over the education of their children. That all authority on a subject so important should be vested in the hands of two or three men of the same way of thinking, seemed to him, at the best, a one-sided arrangement; surely it was more just that a committee of men should be chosen by the votes of the people, and that every form of thought should find its exponent—thus keeping the balance of opinion even. Much more he said, and said it

H. Louisa Bedford

ably, ending with a strong appeal that each one there present, unbiassed by any cry of party, should think out this subject for themselves, and consider whether he was doing the best for the place in which he lived by saying, that what had been should be and could not be improved; or whether he would make use of that power vested in him by Government, and should decide to let his voice, in the education of the future generation, find expression in that great and powerful development of modern times, a School Board.

Allison, forgetful of his fears about rates, murmured "Ooray!" as the squire resumed his seat; and the rector, thanking the squire for his able expression of his views, asked if there were any one else who would give them the benefit of his opinion. There was a long silence. It was hoped that Allison would have something to say and one and another gave him a friendly nudge, but the blacksmith was too wise to commit himself; he halted between two opinions. But there was a murmur of astonishment as Macdonald rose and, supporting his burly form against the wall, cleared his throat, and began to speak a little huskily.

"No, thank you, sir," he said in answer to a nod from the rector to come up to the platform. "I ain't scholard enough to stand up there, but there's something I wants to say. The squire says as we should know our own minds, and I'd like to tell you what's mine. Who should have care of the children but the man who loves 'em like his own, who goes reg'lar to see after 'em every day whilst we goes to work, who teaches 'em to be good at school and to mind what their parents says at home, and wants 'em most of all to love their God? If we voted him out to-night we'd vote him in again to-morrow, and I'll give a pound to-night to show as I'm ready to bide by my words. That's all, gentlemen."

And Macdonald sat down with a very red face, which he

promptly mopped with a redder pocket-handkerchief, whilst Mrs. Macdonald unfolded her clean one and wiped happy tears from her eyes. She dated every event in after life from the night when "my John" made his speech in the school-room. Its effect was electric, and roused the meeting to enthusiasm.

A vote of confidence in the present management was proposed and carried by an overwhelming majority, as seventy hands were counted in support of it, and only five were raised against it. The subscription list lay on the table, and not a few of the working-class, mindful of Macdonald's example came up to enter their names under his.

"I shall make my subscription a hundred pounds, May; I really shall," said Mrs. Webster, feeling that her moral support was taking substantial form. "Poor Mr. Curzon! I think Mr. Lessing's speech was very uncalled-for, and that old Macdonald really surprised me. I thought him a rude old man the only time I spoke to him, but to-night he was simply charming. I felt almost inclined to cry. I'm going to put down my name now. I wish Mr. Curzon to realize that I am on his side, whatever the squire may be;" and Mrs. Webster swept towards the platform.

Left to herself May stood and looked down the room which was emptying rapidly. The squire stood apart but, catching her eye, moved towards her with a slightly satirical smile.

"So you've lived it through, Miss Webster; you've faced the bitter end," he said, quoting her words.

"Yes; and I've not been bored at all," she answered, resenting his tone.

"You came to scoff, in fact, and you remained to pray."

"I came with an open mind, prepared to be converted by the best speaker, and I found him in Macdonald," said May, defiantly. "Henceforth I shall be an ardent supporter of the voluntary system."

Paul laughed. "Will your ardent support take tangible form like old Macdonald's?" he said. He spoke in pure jest, but May accepted his words literally and flushed a little. "It's a question that your very short acquaintance with me hardly justifies you in asking, does it?"

"Not in earnest, certainly; I spoke in the merest fun. If I vexed you, I apologize."

"You did vex me. It is the second time to-night that you have put yourself out of the way to say a disagreeable thing. People may think as many disagreeable things as they like, but they have no right to give expression to them."

"But now you are charging me with sins which I have not committed. I have not spoken to you for five minutes, and no other sentiment of mine, that I know of, needs a special apology."

"A look does! You looked cross as you stooped to unfasten my dress from that nail when I came into the room: it bored you to render me even that very slight service. Pray don't attempt to deny it! you possess the merit of being strictly truthful."

"Truthfully disagreeable apparently," said Paul, a little nettled.

"And now," said May, restored to perfect good-humour by having spoken out her mind, "the platform seems vacant; shall we go and consider that subscription list, or will it hurt your feelings?"

"Not the least. I've suffered defeat, but I was glad of the opportunity of speaking."

"Why?" asked May, as she mounted the platform.

"Because I have won four to my side; I made four people think."

"Then the people who followed Macdonald's lead, which includes myself, are credited with not having the capacity of thinking. That is your inference, is it not?" asked May, with a gay laugh.

"You have a sharp tongue, Miss Webster. All I hinted at was that country people are slow to exercise their individual judgment on any question. They follow each other like a flock of sheep."

"And aren't they wise to do it when they have so kind and good a shepherd?" with a glance at the rector's handsome head, as he stood at a little distance off, talking with a happy, radiant face to her mother. "I wish you would tell me what possible motive you had in trying to upset a man who lives in the hearts of his people."

Paul was interested in spite of himself, for he saw that May had passed from brilliant nonsense to earnestness.

"It was not the man I wished to upset—nobody can fail to appreciate his simple earnestness,—but it is his principle. And your very intolerance makes me feel that I was right to state the other side of the question."

"We won't quarrel any more; I'm tired of it," said May, with a quick change of mood. "Let us look at all the people who are ready to bide by their words, as Macdonald puts it."

The subscription list was headed by the rector with two hundred pounds.

"He's not a rich man," said May, pointing to the sum.

"And he can't be a poor one," retorted Paul.

May seated herself and toyed with the pen which lay upon the table.

"I'm in a difficulty; I want an opinion."

"Legal?" said Paul. "If so, I might help you.

"Moral rather."

"Oh, then it's a case for the man who lives in the hearts of his people. Shall I call him?"

"You are not keeping the peace. For want of a better adviser I'll put my difficulty before you."

"And I will give you my opinion for what it is worth; you need not act on it unless you like."

"Oh no, I shan't. Should you think it right for me to put my name down on this subscription list when I owe, I'm afraid to say how much, to my dressmaker?"

"At the risk of being told again that I'm truthfully disagreeable, I answer emphatically, No! I should call it a most immoral act."

"Well, I'm going to do it anyway, and the person who has influenced me is yourself. You implied that I was unwilling to pay for my convictions; and my dressmaker must wait."

And May dipped her pen in the ink and wrote her name boldly under her mother's.

"Don't do it!" pleaded Paul, hurriedly. "Can't you see that the dressmaker, who earns her money so hardly, and waits for it so long, has the first right to yours?"

"May!" called her mother. "Are you never coming? I can't be kept waiting all night."

May hesitated for a moment, and then, half ashamed of yielding to the man whose dislike of her was fast deepening into contempt, she dashed her pen through the name she had just written, bringing her hand, as she did so, into contact with the lamp upon the table. With a smothered exclamation Paul bent across her and tried to stay its fall, but he was not in time. With a crash it fell forwards breaking the bowl, and a trickling stream of blazing paraffin ran down May's muslin skirt, enveloping her in flame. A piercing shriek from the other end of the room showed that Mrs. Webster realized her daughter's peril, and the rector dashed forward to the rescue; but Paul had already torn his coat from his back, and was holding it closely upon the burning skirt.

"See to the platform! she's safe enough!" he shouted as the rector ran up; and, almost before May realized the extreme danger from which she had been delivered, she was lifted from the platform and laid very gently on the floor.

"What are you putting me on the floor for? I'm not going to faint," she said, with lips that trembled a little. "I'm all right. Don't let mother be frightened."

H. Louisa Bedford

Paul could not but admire the girl's wonderful self-possession.

"And you are not burned? You are sure you are in no way hurt?"

"Thanks to your marvellous quickness, no," she answered.

But Mrs. Webster, tearful but thankful, was at hand, and Paul felt he could not do better than leave May in her mother's charge.

The rector, meanwhile, with one or two others, was successfully battling with the burning stream of paraffin; and in a few minutes all serious fear of a conflagration was over.

"Now we had better see the ladies to their carriage," he said turning to Paul. But already they had taken their departure. "We can't be too thankful for such a narrow escape. The platform looked all on fire when Mrs. Webster's scream made me turn round. Can you tell me how it happened?"

"I think Miss Webster caught the lamp with her hand as she got up from the table. She had been reading the subscription list."

"Which reminds me that the list is burned to a cinder. But it does not signify; people will remember their promises," said Mr. Curzon.

"And nobody but myself will know that May Webster put down her name and scratched it out at my request," thought Paul, not a little proud of his moral victory over the haughty young woman.

"Well, I think everything is safe here; we may be going

home. I want to get back before my little Kitty gets news of the fire, or she will worry herself into a fever. Late as it is, though, I must run up to the Court."

"Why?" Paul inquired. "We know that Miss Webster is safe."

"She might wish to see me," replied the rector, simply. "And if she does, she shall have the chance."

"Then I'll leave word at the rectory that you are all right, in case Kitty is awake," said Paul, rather shortly.

May, from her couch in her dressing-room heard the rector's cheery voice in the hall below asking after her.

"That's Mr. Curzon, Lancaster; run and ask him to come up and see me for a moment," she said to her maid.

In another moment he entered, followed by her mother.

"Oh, my darling, you are not ill? Have you been burned and not told me of it?" she gasped in terror.

"Oh no, mother," said May, trying to smile; "but it's just because I'm not burned, nor scared, nor horrible to look at, that I want Mr. Curzon. I want—I want—" And then May's high courage gave way, and she burst into tears.

"Let us pray," said the rector, quietly. And he and May's mother knelt down by the side of May's couch together.

When he rose up from his knees May's tears had ceased.

H. Louisa Bedford

CHAPTER VII

A MOMENTOUS DECISION

The rector walked home through the starlight night with a thankful heart. It was possibly his sanguine temperament, backed by his strong faith in the Christ Who must reign until He had brought all to His Feet, that gave him such large success in his work; and against the background of this day two special subjects for thanksgiving stood out in strong relief: first, that he had received positive proof that he possessed the confidence of the majority of his parishioners; and secondly, that an accident—a deliverance from what might have been a horrible death—had given him an insight into the deeper side of May Webster's character. That she had this deeper side he had been fully assured, but hitherto he had been powerless to touch it.

To-night, however, she had appealed to him to give expression to the gratitude which she felt to God. For a moment the spiritual life that was in her had touched his, and he trusted that the foundation of a deeper, truer, more lasting friendship had been laid—a friendship that might enable him, possibly, to give May Webster a helping hand on her road to Heaven.

Mr. Curzon was not one of those who believe that a clergyman's mission is fulfilled by looking after the poor who are committed to his care. He had seen enough of society to realize both its fascination and its special temptations; and the well-to-do members of his flock were as frequently included in his prayers as the poor, the afflicted, the sick, or the unhappy.

It was of May and her needs that his heart was full as he turned from the drive into the road, but as he did so he stumbled against a man's figure propped against the gate-post. The man lurched heavily forward, and would have fallen had not Mr. Curzon caught him in his arms, peering at the same time into his face to see who it might be.

"Tom! Tom Burney! Poor lad," he exclaimed, with a heavy sigh, for the mere touch of the inert body showed that Tom was not overcome by illness but by drink.

"Tom!" said the rector, giving him a slight shake of the shoulders, "rouse yourself, and get home to bed. To-morrow we will talk this over, but you are in no fit state to listen to-night."

The familiar voice roused the muddled brain to some sense of shame, and instinctively Tom's hand was raised to his cap.

"Beg your pardon, sir, but I won't go home; same roof shan't cover that beast Dixon and me!"

The words reminded Mr. Curzon that Dixon, Burney, and several other men employed at the Court were lodged in rooms over the coach-house and stables; evidently Tom and Dixon had quarrelled.

"That's sheer nonsense!" he answered sharply. "I'm not going to leave you out here all night, for the sake of your own character. If you won't go without me, I shall take you."

H. Louisa Bedford

Tom made some show of sullen resistance, but a sober man always has the advantage over a tipsy one; and Mr. Curzon was physically so strong that, drunk as Tom was, he knew he could enforce obedience. Once more, therefore, the rector had to retrace his steps, and half supported, half led, he presently landed Tom Burney in the stable-yard of the Court. A light burning in one of the upper windows showed him that somebody was still awake, and a whistle readily attracted the attention of the occupant. The window was thrown wide and a head thrust out into the night.

"So it's you, is it?" said a voice, that the rector recognized as Dixon's. "It would serve you right to keep you out there all night."

"You hound! you mean hound!" hiccoughed Tom, trying to wrest himself from the strong restraining hand laid upon his collar. "If only I can get at you, I'll—"

The threat was nipped in the bud by the rector. "Is that you, Dixon?" he asked, in a low, authoritative tones. "Just come down and open the door, please. I found Burney like this, and brought him home; and keep out of sight, will you? I've no intention of being landed in a quarrel."

There was a smothered exclamation of surprise, the window was closed, and, in another moment, the lower door was thrown wide to admit the rector and his charge. By a rapid signal Mr. Curzon directed Dixon to conceal himself in an angle of the staircase, whilst he gave Tom a helping hand up the staircase to the room which Dixon indicated with a nod. Once safely inside, he placed him on the bed and came away, closing the door behind him.

"He won't come out again to-night, I think," he said to Dixon, who followed him to the door.

"Oh no, sir; I'll see to that," replied the man, with a rather unpleasant smile. "I'll turn the key on him, and unlock the door again before he wakes in the morning. I'm sorry you've had all this trouble. I tried my best to get him to come along quietly with me, but I had to leave him to himself at last; he was so desperate quarrelsome. He's a quick temper at any time, and he's just mad when he's drunk."

"Which has not been very often, I think," interposed the rector. "But in the last few months, I fear he has fallen into bad company. Good night, Dixon."

"We shan't hear the end of this in a hurry. What business has he prowling about the place at this time of night, I should like to know?" grumbled Dixon aloud, as he closed the door. "Bad company, indeed! He'll see for himself that I'm not drunk, whatever that fool Tom may be."

Meanwhile the rector pursued his way home in less joyful mood than before he had stumbled across poor Tom Burney; he was sorely troubled about him as, for a long time, he had been one of the most promising young fellows in the place. He let himself quietly into the rectory, shading the light with his hand as he passed the door of Kitty's room; but a half-stifled cry of "Daddy!" arrested his steps. He pushed open the door and entered, crossing with swift, light tread to her bedside. The frightened look in the child's eyes died away as she looked into the smiling face.

"What does my little Kitty mean by lying awake to this hour?"

"I've been frightened, daddy. I lay awake on purpose, at first, because you promised to come and kiss me when you came home after the meeting."

H. Louisa Bedford

"Oh, I shan't promise that any more if it keeps you awake. Well!"

"And then I heard Mr. Paul's voice down in the hall, and I thought he said something about fire. But Nurse said I was silly, and must go to sleep; but I couldn't till I knew you were safe."

"What from, little one?"

"The fire," said Kitty, with a suppressed sob. "I thought you might be burned, and nobody would tell me."

"Well, that was very silly, certainly," said her father, with a little laugh that had a singularly reassuring effect upon Kitty.

"And I tried to think of the three men with long names that the fire did not hurt; but it did not do me a bit of good, daddy."

"Because you forgot about the fourth one who stood by them, even in the fire, whose form was like the Son of God," said the rector, gently. "And He was close by you, Kitty, although you were so frightened—by you, and me too. There! think of that and go to sleep now."

But though Mr. Curzon spoke so cheerfully, there were tears in his eyes as he kissed his little daughter and tucked her into bed with strong, gentle hands.

"Poor little soul! She's bound to suffer, with her crippled body and over-sensitive brain," he thought.

The next morning at breakfast he told Kitty the story of the previous evening, quite simply, without any terrifying details.

"I should think Mr. Paul is very brave—almost as brave as you are, daddy," said Kitty, whose terror seemed to have vanished into thin air with the light of day.

"Much braver, I expect," agreed her father, good-humouredly. "But I wonder why you think so!"

"Oh, Sally has told me lots of things. How he killed a mad dog, and nursed a man with smallpox, and knocked down a costermonger for kicking his pony. That was brave, wasn't it?" said Kitty, who clearly regarded the last item as the crowning act of bravery.

"Well, it was speedy punishment, certainly," answered her father, laughing. "But since you admire bravery so much, you'll have to learn a little more about it yourself; and not lie awake every time I'm kept out late at night. A clergyman's work is like a doctor's—never done, you know."

The word doctor gave Kitty an opportunity of rapidly changing the subject.

"What's a stroke, father? What's good for it?"

"A 'stroke' generally means paralysis, in some form or other, which affects people's limbs—often making them useless."

"Like my legs?" asked Kitty, quickly.

Her father winced palpably. "Not just like that, darling; I wonder what you are thinking of?"

"Mr. Allison's mother. She's very old and very deaf; and now she's had a stroke. I heard some one tell Nurse so; and, of course, I must go and ask about her when I go out; but I can't tell what to take her."

"I should think beef-tea will be the kind of thing she needs. Nurse can say we will make her some if you like," said the rector, who always humoured Kitty's fancy for taking sick people especially under her wing.

The day was a full one, and it was late in the afternoon before he found himself rapping at the door of the house which adjoined the forge.

"Thank you, sir," said Mrs. Allison, in answer to his inquiry about her mother-in-law; "she's a bit tired to-day, though going on as well as we could hope. She's had a visitor this afternoon," with a glance round at the chimney-corner from which Sally Lessing's tall, girlish figure emerged rather shyly; "and if you did not mind looking in rather earlier to-morrow she'd be ready to see you."

"Very good," said the rector. "If you'll name the time, I'll be here. Miss Lessing, our way home lies in the same direction. Shall we walk together?"

No excuse presented itself for refusing Mr. Curzon's offer, though a *tete-a-tete* with the rector was not much to her taste—especially as her brother was a little sore about his last night's defeat.

"How are you taking to the life down here? Do you like it?" he asked, as they started off together.

"I don't quite know," Sally said with a frank smile. "At first it was delightful—a new experience,—but the novelty is wearing off. And Paul said this morning that we were both of us fish out of water; that he must stay here, at any rate for the present, but that I might please myself."

"And what particular pond do you want to swim in?"

"London. And that's not to be described as a pond, is it? but rather a great, strong river. You see, down here, there is literally nothing to do."

"Plenty, if you choose to do it," replied Mr. Curzon, quietly.

Sally shook her head. "You would only want workers of your own way of thinking."

"I should prefer them, certainly; if by *my* way of thinking you mean the Church to which I belong—to which you belong also, I expect."

"Only by name. I was baptized, but I've not been brought up on church lines. I've been allowed to think for myself, and judge the truth for myself. Paul says that that is the only truth worth believing."

"It still leaves you finally dependent on other people's judgment, does it not? In your case, I should say, your views unconsciously are moulded entirely by your brother."

"But it is so with every one more or less!" retorted Sally, quickly. "You've got your ideas, either from the people who have influenced you the most, or the books you have read."

"Quite so. The books that have influenced me most largely are those contained in the Bible; but the only person upon whose judgment and character I find I can wholly rely, is the Lord Himself. An old-fashioned belief, you will say, but I find it practically true."

"But Paul says the only facts based on history in the Gospels are that Christ lived and died a martyr to his opinions," said Sally.

"So many men say nowadays. If so, it is curious that faith in the Name of a Jew who died nearly two thousand years ago, is still able to work moral miracles in hundreds and thousands of lives in the present day; that men and women, tied and bound with the chain of their sins, looking to Him and asking help, can rise and walk in the glorious liberty of the sons of God. When I see that, as, thank God, I have seen it, I feel I have a reason for the faith that is in me, that Jesus is, as He claims to be, the Son of God; that it was no idle boast on His part that He would give His Spirit to those that seek it."

Sally caught her breath. There was no doubting the sincerity of the speaker, but the very simplicity of the teaching was an argument against accepting it.

"Well, of course, you as a clergyman have to do with people's morals," she said hurriedly; "but the bodily wretchedness and misery of hundreds and thousands of people in London and other big places appeals more to me. I feel it's not a bit of good telling them to be good in this world, and they will be happy in the next, whilst they have bad houses to live in, and bad food to eat, and insufficient wages, and never a ray of brightness in their lives. To stay down here and potter about amongst a few children and sick people seems such a small thing to do, when one might help to set any one of these great wrongs right."

She pulled herself up, and broke into a peal of laughter.

"I'm talking of things that I dare say you will think I don't understand," she said; "but Paul has interested me in them, and I had thought, if I went on studying, I might some day work and speak about them. Lots of women do."

"And why not? One of the best speakers I ever heard was

a woman."

"I thought you would be sure to hate the notion."

"Why should I, unless—"

"Unless what?"

"You should speak any word against the Master whom I serve," said the rector. "On philanthropic subjects I could go with you heart and soul."

"I would not speak on a subject of which I know nothing," said Sally, eagerly. "I've told you that I am only a seeker after truth, picking up a scrap here and there as I can find it."

"And you will reach the truth after a time," said Mr. Curzon, holding out his hand, "if you are ready to acknowledge a Power higher than yourself, to Whom you may safely appeal to guide you to all truth. Without that, you will grope along in the darkness."

Before Sally could answer he had gone. Was there such a power she wondered? What rest and comfort such a conviction would bring with it. She made no mention of her talk to the rector to Paul when he came in; she shrank from his glib criticism of Mr. Curzon's simple declaration of faith.

As Mr. Curzon walked home he caught sight of Tom Burney leaning over a gate with his back turned towards the road. The very poise of his head, and droop of his shoulders, showed depression of body and mind; and with intuitive sympathy Mr. Curzon stopped and laid a kindly hand on his shoulder.

"The very man I was wanting!" he said cheerily. "I thought

H. Louisa Bedford

you would be sure to come and see me to-night."

For a moment Tom's dark, handsome eyes sought his; then dropped for very shame.

"No, I wasn't," he said bluntly. "But I'm glad to have the chance of telling you that I've got the sack for what happened last night. Dixon took good care to report me; and I'm to leave at the end of this week."

"What is your quarrel with Dixon?"

There was a long pause. "We're after the same girl," said Tom, a little huskily; "and he don't care what he does as long as he can get me out of the way. He made me drunk last night."

"Oh no," replied Mr. Curzon, shortly; "you made yourself drunk. Tell the truth about it, Tom."

"Well, I'll tell you straight what happened. We were all in the public together—"

"You went there of your own free will, I suppose?"

"Yes. I've been there plenty of times before, and never had a drop too much," said Tom, rather resentfully, "and I was just going away last night, when Dixon offered me another glass; and Allison laughed and said, 'Don't you take it, young 'un; head ain't strong and temper too short.' And I told him I could drink against any man if I chose, and keep my wits about me too; and Dixon said he'd stand treat, and see whose head would last the longest, mine or Allison's—"

"With the result that I found you how and when I did, and you've lost your place into the bargain. Truly the wages of sin are hard," commented Mr. Curzon; "but I'm ready to help you, Tom, if you are willing to help yourself, for I think, to a certain extent, you've been hardly done by. If you are sorry for what has happened, and really wish to turn over a new leaf, and make yourself worthy of the girl you love, you'll take my advice and sign the pledge. If you see your way to doing this, I know of a situation that I could offer you; if not, I strongly advise you to go away altogether."

"And leave the field clear for Dixon? I'll never do it!" said Tom, fiercely. "And what would he call me but a coward if I signed the pledge, just because I've been beastly drunk once in my life? There's no reason why I should do it again."

"That you will do it again is an absolute certainty; and with your hot temper and the rivalry that exists between you and Dixon, there will be serious mischief if you allow drink to get the upper hand. The place I offer you is that of gardener at the rectory. Old Plumptree is retiring on a pension; he's too old to do the work any longer. But I tell you frankly that I dare not undertake the responsibility of keeping you here unless I feel that you are determined, God helping you, to make a better start. You need not decide in a hurry; you can call to-morrow evening and let me know about it. Until then I will keep the situation open for you."

It was on the tip of Tom's tongue to tell the rector that he needed no time for consideration, that he readily accepted the required condition, and should be thankful for the situation that he offered, when, as ill-luck would have it, Dixon passed by on a swift-trotting horse, and turned upon Tom with a mocking smile.

"He thinks I'm catching it," thought poor Tom; "but I'll let him know better."

"It's not that I'm ungrateful, sir, for your kindness last night, but my mind's pretty well made up now. I can't face Dixon and Allison, and all the lot of 'em calling me a fool who can't take his glass without getting drunk; I'll show 'em different. But I'll promise you this: it's the first time as any one of em, sneaks as they are, could tell you that I'd been drunk, and it's the last too! You shall hear no more of it."

"And it's a promise that I tell you honestly you'll not keep," answered Mr. Curzon, sadly. "But you'll think it over; you won't decide until to-morrow."

"Yes, sir; I've made up my mind, thank you kindly all the same," said Tom. "It's a thing I must settle for myself."

"Good night, then; I've nothing more to say except that at any time if you are in trouble I shall be glad to see you. I don't wish you to think that this difference of opinion need separate us; although, remember, I feel sure that I am right and you wrong."

The next morning, when Paul Lessing started for his walk, Tom Burney stood waiting at the gate.

"Beg your pardon, sir," he said, touching his hat; "but I want to know if you can give me work?"

Paul turned to the speaker with dawning recognition in his glance.

"Why, aren't you the fellow who gave me a lift for nothing the first evening I came into the place."

"Yes, sir; I've often thought on it since. I shouldn't have spoke so free if I'd known who I was talking to."

"Why not?" said Paul, smiling pleasantly. "You sent me to the proper person to find me a lodging, at any rate; and you certainly spoke no harm of any one. I thought you told me you worked at the Court.

"So I did, sir; but I'm leaving there on Saturday."

"Of your own free will?"

"Not exactly; I got notice because I came home drunk one night."

"Is that your habit, may I ask? It's a bad one."

"No, sir, it's not," said Tom, lifting fearless eyes. "It was the first time."

"Let it be the last, then. What kind of work can you do?"

"I've been in the garden; but I know something about horses."

"Well, I'm going to take the management of the home farm that lies near the Court, into my own hands, and I think I can find you work amongst the horses. I'll see the bailiff about it, and you can call on Saturday night, when we will settle the question of wages."

Tom's heart gave a joyful throb! A place on the farm close to the Court would give him opportunities of many a stolen interview with Rose; and if he showed himself willing and ready to do the thing that came to his hand, he might rise to the position of bailiff before very long, and find himself able to give his Rose as pretty a home as she could wish for.

"I won't forget your kindness, nor how you're ready to take

H. Louisa Bedford

me without a character. I'll serve you honest and true," he said.

"It is only one more example of the capriciousness of rich people," said Paul, as he told the tale to Sally later in the day. "Here was this poor fellow dismissed without a character for what I honestly believe was a first offence. I'm glad to give him a helping hand."

But Paul was judging hastily; Tom Burney had received notice from the gardener, who had not thought it worth while to consult Mrs. Webster about the matter.

CHAPTER VIII

AN OUTSTRETCHED HAND

It was many weeks before Paul and May Webster met after the night of the fire. The Court was crammed with company, and although Paul and his sister were invited to dinner more than once, such invitations were politely declined.

"It's quite impossible, Sally," Paul had said, in answer to the rather wistful look in her dark eyes. "To dine there quietly by ourselves, is one thing; to go and meet a heap of smart people, who are my special abomination, is another; and I should not have thought you would have wished it either."

"It would be so much experience; I could be in it but not of it. But I expect I should not be smart enough, either in my dress or my talk; so we must decline, I suppose. What shall I say?"

"Anything you like within the limits of truth."

"Paul won't come, and I can't because I have not a proper frock," said Sally, merrily. "I am sorry, and he is not."

"Don't talk nonsense, Sally," said Paul, with an answering laugh. "Any woman can write a decent note of refusal if

H. Louisa Bedford

she chooses."

So the decent note was written and despatched, to be followed by another, rather differently worded, when the second invitation came about a week later, after which they were asked no more. Sally watched the smart carriages drive to and from the station, with their varying loads of visitors, with a passing pang of regret. It was like gazing into a shop-window when you are possessed of no money to buy the tempting wares displayed there.

Paul scarcely gave his gay neighbours a thought; his head was full of plans for the improvement of the place, and it fretted him a little that on every hand he found himself unable to carry out his wishes for the want of the necessary means.

He was not altogether popular: the poor people rather resented the extreme simplicity of his manner of living when they discovered that it was not accompanied by the open-handed liberality which Allison had half led them to expect; the tenant-farmers opposed any change that would touch their pockets; and people of his own class, few and far between in that thinly populated neighbourhood, called once, but found little to interest them in a man of such avowedly eccentric views on things social and religious, and tacitly let the acquaintance drop.

The one exception to this was May Webster, who, half-piqued, half-amused, at the barrier which Paul had chosen to erect between them, determined to break it down. She was coming out of the rectory one afternoon when she met him at the gate.

He lifted his hat, and would have opened the gate to let her pass, but she held it fast looking at him over the top.

"How are you? It is long since we met; never, I think, since the night of the meeting with its exciting close. I've not thanked you properly, by the way, for the rapid extinction of the flames."

"Oh, any one could have done it; only I happened to be the one nearest you," said Paul, carelessly. "It needs no special thanks."

"Which is a civil way of saying that you could not let me burn, but that you would rather some one else had put me out," said May, mockingly. "Even so, I'm grateful; I've been calling on your friend Kitty, who informed me with great triumph that daddy was out, but 'Mr. Paul' was coming to tea with her. Questioned further, she informed me that he often came when she was by herself, and he said he liked it."

"So I do," Paul said.

"So tea fetches you if dinner does not; or perhaps it is not the meal, but the company. Frankly speaking, why do you accord your friendship to Kitty and not to mother and me? We may be neighbours for years and years; we may just as well be friends."

"I'm not a man of many friends," Paul answered, fairly brought to bay. "As for Kitty, she carried me by storm; she is the only child who has taken to me of her own free will."

"How very odd," said May, thoughtfully.

"Oh yes; I admit the oddity."

"But, if you are going to live here, are you content to be isolated from your fellows—to have no friends?" continued May, wonderingly.

"To have many acquaintances seems to me a dreary waste of life; and the word friendship, in the mouth of a man, implies many things."

"Notably what?" asked May, a little scornfully.

"Similarity of tastes and thought."

"And, I suppose, no one down here is clever enough for you?"

"I hope I'm not such an intolerable prig as to have implied that. But, frankly, I expect that you and I, for instance, would not take the same view on any subject; and, very likely, the things that interest me would bore you to extinction."

"It would bore me pretty considerably if you persisted in urging that the whole world should be reduced to one level of ugly uniformity, which is what you are credited with believing."

"A free interpretation of a hope, on my part, to lessen the cruel gulf between the very rich and the very poor," replied Paul, quietly. "I confess, the frightful extravagance of the wealthier classes makes me sick at heart; for one section of society nothing but amusement and pleasure, and the lavish spending of money; and for the larger half the weary effort to make both ends meet—and for many quiet, hopeless starvation."

"You are talking something like the rector; only he enlists my sympathy more by speaking less severely—and he is more just too. He does not talk as if it were wicked to be better off than your neighbour; he only makes you feel the responsibility of it."

Paul gave rather a hard little laugh.

"To speak plainly, he dresses it up a little—gives it the clerical dash of sentiment. Besides, what is the good of stirring one here and there to give out of his abundance something of which he will never feel the loss, with the comfortable sense left behind that he or she has done something very big indeed. What one would strive for, rather, is to stir up the nation to its duties, to rouse Government to redress some of these glaring social grievances."

"Oh, pray keep yourself in hand! level your intellect down to mine!" cried May, with a burst of laughter. "As far as I follow you, you wish to lower my dress allowance by act of parliament. I sincerely trust you will fail. By the way you may set your mind at rest about my dressmaker; her bill is paid, and all my other outstanding accounts too. With your rather eccentric views about property, it will annoy you considerably to hear that I have had a fortune left me; so that I may not be in debt again for some considerable time."

"To her that hath," said Paul, with a glance at the elegantly clad figure. "It really seems to me as if you could not want it, and I need it so much."

"You!" echoed May. "For real inconsistency commend me to yourself!"

"I scarcely require it for my personal wants, but money is sorely needed to carry out my wishes for this village. As landlord, I feel myself responsible for many things that cannot be set right without it."

"But—but—mother always told me that Major Lessing was rich; and you are his heir."

"I can only assure you that I am poor," said Paul, simply. "Now, I hope, I have proved satisfactorily to you that circumstances, tastes, and opinions differing so greatly between us, make anything like friendship impossible. Whenever we come across each other we quarrel; we can't help it."

May flushed to the roots of her hair. "Thank you," she said haughtily. "It is kind of you to put it so clearly. I simply tried to put things on a kinder footing, as we are your tenants and your neighbours, but I see I have made a mistake. It surprises me to find you so painfully prejudiced. Good-bye. I've kept you too long from your one friend."

She opened the gate and passed on her way with never a look behind; but Paul followed with long, rapid strides.

"Miss Webster! stay one moment, please! I believe I've been behaving like a perfect brute," he said hurriedly. "At first I thought you were simply playing a game with me; but, without knowing it, we drifted into earnestness. If any word of mine has seriously vexed you, I apologize and retract."

"You could even believe it possible that I might feel a ray of interest in some of the big subjects which absorb your life," said May.

"To have made a man acknowledge himself a prig once in an afternoon is enough," retorted Paul. "I will not do it again. You know the worst of me: that I have an uncertain temper, which betrays me occasionally into blurting out unpleasant truths: that I have absolutely no small talk. I shall be at best but a rough-and-ready friend; but if in your kindness you still care to cultivate Sally and me, we will gratefully accept the cultivation, and be the better for it. There's my hand on it," and Paul stretched out his hand. And May gave him her small gloved one for an instant with a very sunny smile.

"And you will come to dinner soon and not feel you need talk down to us."

"When all the smart people have gone," Paul said smiling.

"Smart people are your pet aversion, apparently. Is that why you would not come lately?"

"Yes; if you wish to hear the truth," Paul admitted as he turned back to the rectory.

"And I have made a pretty big fool of myself this afternoon," was his mental comment as he let the gate clang behind him. "I first lost my temper, and then let a woman twist me round her finger simply because she is beautiful."

Needless to relate he made no confession of his folly to Sally when he got home that night. He resolved simply to change his tactics about the people at the Court, and preserve safe silence about his altered mind.

The following afternoon he stopped at the forge to speak to the blacksmith about some repairs that were to be set on foot on his premises. Allison stood at the open door of the smithy with his head turned in the opposite direction from the squire, looking after the rector, who had just left him, with something of the sullen satisfaction with which a bulldog might regard a vanquished foe. Indignation still simmered when Paul accosted him. One glance at the purple face showed the squire that, for some reason as yet unknown, the blacksmith was in a towering passion.

"Confound his impudence!" he said, throwing a dark look after the rector. "I've let him know once for all that I'll have no more of it! I'm not answerable to him, nor any man, for what I says and does. His business, indeed, to come and tell me, if I choose to have a bit of fun with a young fellow in a public-house. What does it hurt him to be drunk for once in his life? A lesson I call it! just a bit of a lesson as will teach him that his head ain't so strong as mine, nor likely to be till he gets seasoned a bit. I give it him straight enough, and no humbug about it. 'Look here, sir,' I says, 'you go your way, and leave me to go mine. I don't deny as you've been kind to my old mother, and she'd fret sore if she didn't see you. Psalm-singing and such comes natural-like to most women; but for my part I want nothing better than to be letted alone.'"

Allison came to a stop; breath rather than words had failed him. Paul, who had been an unwilling listener to this tirade against the rector, took advantage of the pause to turn the subject.

"Afraid I can't attend to you this afternoon sir," said Allison, when Paul stated the object of his call. "Reason why, my mates are out for a holiday, and this mare here is just brought in to be shod. I said at first I would not do her to-day; she's a savage brute to tackle alone. I don't let any one touch her but myself when the men are here. It's wonderful now what a difference there is in the tempers of horses; but I ain't come across the one I couldn't master in the forge. They feel I ain't afeared on 'em."

Boasting of his prowess in his art was fast restoring Allison's temper, which, though violent, was not enduring.

"Very well; I'll come again to-morrow," said Paul.

"And you'll thank missy for lookin' up my mother as she does," said Allison, referring to Sally's visits to the old lady, his mother. "She's one as it does you good to see, so pleasant and free-spoken. Now some on 'em," with a glance in the direction of the Court, "don't look as if they thought you good enough to black their shoes, and that don't do for me."

"She does not do herself justice," thought Paul, as he walked away, unconsciously taking up the cudgels in May Webster's defence; "she can be gracious enough when she chooses. She has insisted on our being friends, and I'll make use of the privilege to tell her the impression she conveys, before many weeks are passed. Allison is a shrewd fellow, and in his blundering fashion knocks many a right nail on the head."

* * * * * *

The October afternoon was fading into night before Paul returned to the cottage. The curtains of the sitting-room were still undrawn, and from within he caught the cheerful glow of the fire, and Sally seated on the rug before it reading by the fitful light. She sprang to her feet as she heard his footstep, and ran to open the door; and then her merry greeting checked itself in the utterance, for her brother's face was grey with suppressed feeling, and his teeth chattered slightly.

"What is it, Paul?" she asked, in a half-frightened whisper.

"It's that poor fellow, Allison; he's dying. And I happened to pass when the accident occurred, and gave a hand in carrying him upstairs. It's ghastly to see a man in mortal agony."

"What happened?"

"A troublesome mare took to kicking as he shod her, and somehow Allison was knocked down; and, before any one could get to the rescue, he was so injured that the doctor does not think he can last through the night."

H. Louisa Bedford

"How awful! And were you there to see it all?" Sally asked with a shiver.

"I had not left the forge very long. I had been talking to Allison, and he told me the mare was a skittish one to manage; and, as I returned, I found a group of men gathered around him, not one of whom had even had the sense of thinking of fetching the doctor. So I first helped them to get poor Allison to his room, and then I rushed to the inn, got a trap, and went and brought a doctor back with me. There is absolutely nothing to be done; but it is a satisfaction to feel that a doctor has seen him. Taken right way, he's not half a bad sort, Sally. He's bearing his pain like a man, and shook me by the hand to bid me good-bye, and even sent a message to you. 'Say good-bye to missy. I'd like to have said it myself,'" he said.

"He shall! I'll go and see him," Sally said, with a set white face. "If the sight of me can give him the smallest pleasure, I'll go."

"It's rather awful, Sally; you've not had to face death yet. I would not go if I were you."

"We all must face it some time or other. I'll go, Paul; I shan't be long. No! don't come with me, please; I'd rather go alone."

"Put on a waterproof, then, and take an umbrella; it's a wild night, and it has just come on to rain," said Paul, and, moved by an unwonted impulse, he stooped and kissed her.

The door of the blacksmith's house was open when Sally reached it, and, entering softly, she removed her wet cloak and stood in the dimly lighted parlour wondering how she should make her presence known. From overhead came the sound of voices talking in suppressed whispers, and once

Sally shivered, for a long-drawn moan fell upon her ear.

"I'll go and see the old mother. Perhaps I can stay with her, and set Mrs. Allison free when I have just said good-bye to her husband," thought Sally, as she went up the stairs.

A near neighbour met her at the top.

"We're just at our wits' end, miss," she said in answer to Sally's inquiry. "The old lady's not to be told anything about it, and Mrs. Allison, poor soul! falls out of one faint into another, and can't stay in the room along with him who's dying."

"May I go to him for a minute. He wanted to see me," said Sally, with a sob.

But, ushered into the chamber of death, Sally stood for a moment overpowered by an awful terror: a chill which seemed as if it would stop the beating of her heart, a terror she could not have explained. Face to face with death! The words were familiar enough, but they had conveyed little meaning to her. This man, who lay there, unable from time to time to keep back a groan of agony, with the grey shadow deepening on his face, and the drops of perspiration standing on his forehead, would soon lie there silent and still, capable of neither speech, nor feeling, nor hearing. He would be simply an empty shell. It was awful!—inexpressibly awful. It all flashed through Sally's mind in one shuddering instant; the next, she had pulled herself together and crossed to the bedside on tip-toe, and stood looking down at the poor, prostrate form with ineffable pity in her dark eyes.

"Oh, Lord! I can't bear it!" broke in a sort of wail from the blue lips. "It can't last long; an hour or so will settle it."

H. Louisa Bedford

The words Sally recognized as an exclamation rather than a prayer, but they brought the rector to her remembrance. If any man could help another in his last agony surely it would be he.

"Mr. Allison," she said, laying her soft hand on the grimy one that moved up and down so restlessly upon the counterpane, "I heard you wanted to see me. Let me do something. Is there no one else you would like to see? Shall I fetch Mr. Curzon?"

Allison's eyes unclosed, dimmed already by the gathering haze of death.

"Bless you, missy; this ain't no place for you, though it's good of you to come. Good-bye. God bless you! You get home again; it will hurt you to see me suffer."

Once more that half-blind appeal to the Higher Power of which Mr. Curzon had spoken, and he spoke with no uncertain sound. He seemed to know about it.

"Won't the rector come?" asked Sally again.

But Allison shook his head.

"No, no; we'd words to-day. I can't mind what about; but it don't matter much. I told 'un not to come."

But as he spoke a step fell on the stair, and the next moment Mr. Curzon pushed open the door with an expression on his face so pitiful, so strong, that in the tension of her feeling, Sally could only sob, and, withdrawing her hand, slip quietly away to the window.

The rector knelt down, bringing his face to a level with the dying man's.

"Allison, dear fellow, I only heard this minute what had happened; and I came. Will you let me stay?"

"You can please yourself," said Allison; "but you can't want to be here. We quarrelled, you and I."

"Not I," said the rector, gently.

"I'm mortal bad! I'm dying!" gasped the blacksmith. "It can't do no good to watch me."

"You'll let me say a psalm or read a prayer."

"No. Where's the use? I wouldn't say 'em living and I can't listen now I'm dying. I ain't no worse than others, and I'm better than some; and what's to see on the other side, I'll learn soon enough for myself. I'm nearly there."

"But God is here! close to you, Allison," pleaded the rector; "asking you even now to turn to Him, to look Him in the Face!"

Sally's breath came in fitful gasps; she looked round the room half expecting the visible shining of that Presence. Instead, the wind sobbed in the chimney and the rain dashed against the window-pane. Death was here, and darkness; but no God, thought Sally.

The rector's hands covered his face, and through his fingers Sally saw that great tears forced themselves in the agony of his wrestling for that soul with God.

"You can please yourself," said Allison, opening his eyes again. "It will do no good, but it won't do harm." And the

H. Louisa Bedford

rector, catching at the feeble flicker of a dawning faith, said the twenty-third Psalm slowly on his knees: "'Though I walk through the valley of the shadow of death, I fear no evil, for Thou art with me—'"

A movement from the dying man made him pause and look up.

"I can't see nothing; give me a grip of your hand. Hold tight; I'm mortal cold."

He did not speak again. Neighbours came and went, moistening the dying lips with brandy; but the eyes had no gleam of recognition in them. For an hour or more the rector sat with the great hand clasped tightly between his own, repeating gently prayer or hymn, no word of which, he feared, could reach the numbed brain, but certain that the Great God in Heaven was looking down upon the sheep that had wandered so far from Him, but whom He still claimed as His own. And Sally waited, too, until the rector rising, bent and softly closed the eyes. Then she knew that Allison was dead, and, slipping from the room, made her way swiftly home, unconscious of the rain that beat upon her head, filled only with the remembrance of the scene she had just witnessed.

"He's dead," she said, when Paul let her in; "he's dead—whatever that may mean. It does not mean going out like a candle—I'm certain it does not mean that,—it means going somewhere else; and, if any one can teach me, I must find out where. I could not die like that, Paul; it's despairing, it's quite hopeless! I'm thankful that I'm young; that I have time to learn. If there's no hope, no light, the mere thought of dying would be enough to drive one mad."

"My poor child! I did wrong to let you see anything so

painful," Paul said, gathering her into his arms. "I am afraid there is no one who can tell you about these things. Nobody knows; that is the sad part of it."

"Mr. Curzon can," said Sally, lifting her head from Paul's shoulder. "He has got hold of something that you and I have missed. There is positive conviction written on his face of the living God whom Allison in dying was vaguely feeling after."

"Oh, he's a fine fellow in his way, I don't deny it, and has the courage of his opinions; but he can't know. Nobody does," said Paul, doggedly. "And now, dear, we'll have supper. You will take a less hysterical view of life and death in the morning."

CHAPTER IX

A CRISIS IN A LIFE

A year had passed since poor Allison's sun set so stormily. It was curious that his death marked the beginning of a new life for Sally; but so it was. It had changed her attitude of mind towards things eternal, from one of placid indifference to active inquiry. Paul's assertion that "nobody knew" satisfied no longer, and she turned from him to Mr. Curzon.

"Death can't be the end of it all," she said abruptly to the rector, when she met him a few days after Allison had passed away.

"Oh no," he answered, following her lead with quick sympathy. "Our Lord's death and resurrection teach us that it is but the beginning."

"I wish I could believe it. Can you help me? can any one help me?" Sally said.

"I may be the signpost to show you the road, and I will tell you of the things which have helped me on the road; but God is even now drawing you to Himself by His Holy Spirit," said Mr. Curzon, earnestly.

Thus, under Mr. Curzon's guidance, Sally began the course of study which ended, before many months had passed away, in the passionate conviction that in Christ alone could be found the Way, the Truth, and the Life.

Paul guessed at the fact that his sister was passing through some new phase of thought, by the books he found left about the room, and by a newly developed earnestness which underlay her natural gaiety of manner.

"Poor child! Allison's death frightened her. And it is as well that she should study both sides of the question," he thought. He did not doubt that eventually she would accept his decision as final.

It was November, and Paul came into lunch one day with an unusual air of depression. His farming venture was proving a grievous failure, as far as money was concerned. On every side he found himself hampered by poverty. The summer had been a wet one, and, in common humanity, he had had to make a considerable reduction in his farm rents; improvements in his cottage property had led to an outlay for which he well knew he could receive no adequate interest, and, as he had tramped over the sodden land this morning, he had been occupied with the anxious consideration how best to make both ends meet.

The longer he lived at Rudham the less he liked it. He was deprived of the society of men of his own way of thinking; and with the rector, who in theory he cordially respected and liked, he found himself nearly always in tacit opposition. Paul's friendship with Kitty was the only connecting link between him and the rector; otherwise they would have drifted hopelessly apart before now. Then, on this particular morning, as he returned home he heard a rumour that May Webster was going to be married to a baronet who had

H. Louisa Bedford

haunted the Court pretty frequently during the last few months; and the hint had filled Paul with unreasoning irritation. Not that it mattered to him whom she married, he assured himself; but the Court had become the one bright spot to him in all the place.

Paul, having promised his friendship, had given it unstintingly, and had been proud to discover that in many of the subjects which interested him the most deeply, he had found May Webster a ready pupil; and when she differed from him she held her own with such merry defiance, that it gave her an added charm in his eyes. And now this mindless, fox-hunting squire was to carry her off, and life at Rudham would sink into one dead level of dulness. Thus it happened that he came home in a captious mood.

"What's the excitement, Sally? A wedding, I suppose, for the bells are making row enough to wake the dead."

"No, it's the Bishop," said Sally, flushing a little. "There is a Confirmation here to-day."

Paul's eyes travelled from Sally's crimsoning face to the white dress she wore.

"I can't see why the Bishop is to be welcomed like a bride, and you are to dress like one of his bridesmaids," he said. "What a singularly inappropriate garment for this dreary November day."

"I am going to be confirmed, Paul."

A long pause followed. It was the crowning vexation of a tiresome morning; but Paul did not wish to say anything that he would afterwards regret.

"It's a decided step, Sally; I wonder if you have thought it over enough? You will probably wake up from this religious craze to find yourself bound down to a creed which your reason rejects."

"It is conviction, not a craze," said Sally. "I have thought about little else for a whole year, and my mind is quite made up."

"Very well, then; I have nothing more to say. You are of age, and must decide such things for yourself; but you've sprung it upon me somewhat suddenly, Sally. I suppose it was by Mr. Curzon's advice that you kept your change of opinion dark?"

"Oh dear no! he wished me to tell you weeks ago. But I've been so happy, I cared so much, I felt as if I could not discuss things with any one who differed from me."

"Then we won't discuss it," Paul said, drawing a long breath. "What time does the thing come off? I'll go down and order the fly; I can't let you walk up to church like that."

"May is going to call for me; she is coming to the service."

"Miss Webster!" said Paul, with a rather incredulous laugh. "I should not have thought it was at all in her line."

"She's glad; she thinks I'm right," said Sally, gently.

It was on the tip of Paul's tongue to ask Sally if she had heard anything of May's rumoured engagement to Sir Cecil Bland; but some fear lest the answer should be in the affirmative held him back. When the carriage from the Court drew up at the gate, he went down to put Sally in, and was rewarded by a friendly nod and smile from May.

H. Louisa Bedford

"Aren't you coming, too?" she asked boldly. "It would make Sally so happy if you did."

Paul shook his head. "I don't understand these things; I leave them to those that do."

"I promise to bring her back safely, and I am coming to tea," went on May, gliding over his refusal. "I've never seen that new wing of yours since it was finished. Cottage, indeed! I call it quite a mansion!" with a glance at the addition which had been lately built on to the Macdonald's house, making it about double its original size.

"A mansion you would not care to inhabit, I expect; but it will do capitally for Sally and me," said Paul.

"I'll decide that when I've seen it. Good-bye, then, till we meet later. Tell Dixon to drive to the church, please."

Paul gave the order, and went back to his new sitting-room, seating himself before his office table, as he called the one which was placed in the bow window. He opened his business ledgers, and congratulated himself on the fact of having a long, quiet afternoon of undisturbed work before him; but one more trivial interruption occurred before he was entirely left to himself. Mrs. Macdonald knocked at the door and stood before him arrayed in her Sunday best.

"Shall you be wanting anything, sir?"

"Nothing whatever, Mrs. Macdonald."

"If not, I would like to go to the church to see Miss Sally and the Bishop. I'd slip out quiet before the end, so as not to keep the ladies waiting for their tea."

"Go by all means," said Paul, smiling a little over the commotion created by a Bishop and his lawn sleeves, and a flock of girls in white dresses and caps.

Then his thoughts reverted to Sally's face, with its sweet seriousness of expression, as she had started for the church, and from Sally he passed on to May; and there his mind lingered. She was beautiful—beautiful beyond compare; and to-day there had been an added grace of tenderness in her manner to Sally: a protecting, motherly care, as if she would shield her from his want of sympathy. She seemed so much older than Sally, and yet there were but four years between them.

He pictured the room as it would appear when she entered it, and he settled which of the two easy-chairs he would draw nearer to the fire, and where he would sit himself, so that he could watch the firelight playing on her face; and then—He covered his face with his hands and shut out the light, the better to understand the cause of the fierce pain that was gnawing at his heart.

It did not take him long to discover what had happened. He, Paul Lessing, a man who had knocked about the world and had mixed with all sorts and conditions of men and women, whose pulses had hitherto never quickened their beating at the touch of a woman's hand or the sound of a voice, found himself, at thirty-one, as helplessly and ridiculously in love as any lad of twenty.

With a smothered exclamation, he pushed back his chair, and began a restless walk up and down the room. Was ever a grown man guilty of such egregious folly before? A great gulf separated him and the woman of his dreams: a gulf that could never be bridged over. In tastes and in circumstances they were separated far as the poles. His love was perfectly

H. Louisa Bedford

hopeless; and yet the notion of her marrying another, and removing herself entirely out of his reach, was intolerable to him. But, as an effectual cure of his madness, he knew that it was the best thing that could happen to him. The remedy was a sharp one, but it would be complete.

"A few days must settle it, and, until then, I need not meet her," said Paul, aloud. "I won't stay in this afternoon; business can take me to the farm."

In another minute he had gone into the village street, almost deserted this afternoon, for most of the villagers had wandered up to the church. Paul's road lay in the same direction; and he walked along with rapid strides, his head bent upon his breast, his heart busied with his new discovery, and the thought how best to live it down. He was mingling with the crowd now, that had gathered round the church-gate waiting for the procession of clergy that was just filing out of the church. From inside came the throb of the organ and the sound of singing; but Paul went upon his way, neither lifting his head nor staying his steps, when a familiar voice close at hand arrested his attention.

"Mr. Paul! I'm so glad you've come! I *can't* see anything; lift me up, please!"

Paul started as he saw that he had nearly tumbled over his friend Kitty, whose invalid carriage was drawn up as near to the gate as possible.

"Poor Kitty! And you want to look at the Bishop and his lawn sleeves, and the girls in their caps, like all the rest of the village," he said, bending over and lifting her high in his strong arms.

"Yes. I suppose you've come to see the Bishop too?" said

Kitty, with a sigh of contentment. "He's very nice, indoors; but oh! he's lovely when he's got his scarlet coat on. But daddy says I must not think about the clothes, but about all the boys and girls whom he will bless to-day. They'll promise to be good, you know."

"Hush! hush!" said Paul, for the procession was upon them. And Kitty, carried away by the thrill of the voices, steadied herself in Paul's arms by clasping hers about his neck, and sang lustily with the rest—

"'Till with the vision glorious
Her longing eyes are blest,
And the great Church victorious
Shall be the Church at rest.'"

The last clergyman in the procession before the Bishop was the rector, and Paul could not but be struck by the singular beauty of his look, the joyous ring of his voice. The "vision glorious" was his at that moment; fresh soldiers had just been sworn in to that great army, whose Captain was Christ, and, though some might fall away, there were many whom he prayed would die fighting. That, and more than that, was written clearly on the rector's face.

"Did you see him? Did you see him?" whispered Kitty, eagerly. "Isn't he beautiful?"

"Yes," said Paul, absently, as he put Kitty back into her carriage. But whilst Kitty referred to the Bishop, Paul spoke of the rector.

Then he hurried on his way, anxious not to encounter Sally or May. The brief interval of sunshine was over, and wreaths of mist gathered along the banks of the river, creeping gradually to the slopes above it, dissolving into fine thick

H. Louisa Bedford

rain as the afternoon darkened into night. And still Paul lingered about his business at the farm, until he felt assured that all danger of coming across May was over: a conviction justified by the fact that he met the carriage from the Court, driving home as he returned to the village, catching a glimpse of a lady's figure inside it.

"How long has May been gone?" he asked, with studied carelessness, as he let himself into he cottage and saw a girl's figure seated on the rug before the fire.

"She's not gone! she's here, wondering why her host was so rude as to absent himself this afternoon. Since when, by the way, have you done her the honour to call her by her Christian name?" And May Webster rose from her lowly position and faced Paul with laughter in her eyes.

Paul felt himself caught at a thorough disadvantage; he was dripping with rain and covered with mud, and, confronted thus suddenly with the girl of whom his heart was full, his usual readiness of speech deserted him.

"You! you!" he stammered. "But I saw you drive by me not a quarter of an hour ago."

"And thought you had timed your homecoming so as judiciously to miss me," said May, mercilessly. "It must have been my mother; she has been spending the day at Fairfield. I told Dixon not to come back for me as I would walk home: a premature decision, for it has rained ever since, and I've been waiting for it to clear up. However, I can wait no longer; and Sally has just gone to forage out a waterproof and umbrella."

"I'll go up to the Court and tell them to send back the carriage," said Paul, preparing to depart.

"No, thank you; I will walk."

"The village fly, then?"

"It, or rather its horse, has had more than its proper work to-day. It is probably now conveying the Bishop to the station."

"I shall come with you, then; it will be quite dark before you get home."

"I'm not afraid of it. I believe you are; there's a queer, scared look about you, as if you had seen a ghost; you still think I was in that carriage. Sally," turning to the girl who had just re-entered the room, "will you tell your brother that I don't wish him to see me home? He's very damp and miserable now."

"And at the risk of being a little damper, I will come; it's ridiculous to argue the point."

With all her boasted independence May was not sorry for Paul's escort when she stepped out into the night. The rain was descending in a steady down pour, the wind came sighing up the valley, and the river swept on its way, lapping against the bark with a dreary, sobbing sound. They walked on in silence side by side until May broke it with an impatient laugh.

"The dreariness of the night has infected us both. You are not often dull. You are always either amusing or interesting. Talk, please."

"I can't talk. I've not an idea in my head except that, if the river gets much higher, there will be a flood, and no more Rudham! And personally, I should not care much if it swept it away and me with it."

"You do yourself injustice; you are very interesting. Why this fit of the blues? You are going to be ill, I expect; you looked rather ill when you came in just now."

"Not a bit of it," said Paul, with a little laugh; "draggled and wet, but not ill. Do you remember that you told me once, a year ago, that I was isolating myself from my fellows? Then I felt as if I could defy that isolation. To-day I have been conscious of it; Robinson Crusoe on his desert island could not feel more utterly lonely. I have been kicking against the pricks, wondering why I am condemned to a life and a place which I hate."

"You have no business to complain of a solitude which you have created yourself."

"Oh no; I blame no one."

"And you have Sally—"

"I *had* Sally. She was my disciple and satellite; but now I shall always be having to take care that I don't hurt her feelings. The slippered ease of the old relationship is dead; I can't talk out to her."

"But you can talk out to me as much as you like. I shan't agree with you; but my faith, such as it is, is not new-born like Sally's. I wish it were half as strong."

Only under cover of the dark would May have dared to say as much.

"No, I can't even talk to you; the friendship is dead too. That was the ghost I saw this afternoon; it would have been a short-lived joy, any way, for I hear you are going to leave Rudham."

"You are talking in riddles now!" cried May. "What should kill our friendship? and where am I going to?"

"To Fairfield; so rumour says."

May stopped short in her walk, and Paul heard her breath coming unevenly. When she spoke again her voice was low, but angry.

"You outstrip the limits of friendship in daring to tell me what the gossips here say of me."

"I had no intention of telling you. I suppose it slipped out because I hate to believe it true."

"You need not believe it; I am not going to marry Sir Cecil Bland," said May, coldly. "What has it to do with you, may I ask?"

"Thank Heaven!" muttered Paul, under his breath.

"What have you against him?"

"Nothing. Except that I suppose he loves you, and I love you too, and, although I know better than you can tell me, that my love is perfectly hopeless, I can bear it if I may let you live in my heart a little while, as the one woman in all the world to me, the only woman I have ever loved or ever wished to marry. That must not have been if you were pledged to marry some one else."

"Oh, stop!" said May, laying an entreating hand upon his arm; "I feel as if I had been so cruel, I would not rest until I had you for a friend, but I never dreamed of this."

"Nor I, until to-day," said Paul. "But when I heard that some one else was likely to marry you I knew."

"Put me back into the old niche. Can't we forget about to-night?"

Paul laughed a little harshly.

"Forget!" he echoed drearily. "How little women know the way a man can love? With you I shall only rank as one of the many moths that have singed their wings by flying too closely about you."

"No, no! I shall think of you always as my one man-friend, to whom I could say anything that was in my head. I shall miss him dreadfully."

"And under no circumstances can you think of me in a different light?"

"I don't know, but I think not," May said simply. "You may think it odd, or call me heartless, but I have not yet met the man I wish to marry. There! you see I trust you to the last. Good-bye, my friend."

Paul bent over the hand that was put into his own and kissed it, and went home feeling that the chill of the night had closed about his heart.

CHAPTER X

RIVAL SUITORS

"Where have you been, May? I have been frightened to death about you."

The process was apparently a painless one, judging from the extreme comfort of Mrs. Webster's surroundings: her easy-chair drawn close to the fire but sheltered from it by a screen, the lamp on the table adjusted to a nicety behind, the illustrated papers ready cut for use, and the last new novel lying open on her lap. May seated herself leisurely and stretched out her hands to the blaze before she answered.

"I've been having tea at the cottage."

"And came home in the wet and dark by yourself?"

"No. Mr. Lessing saw me home."

"Of course; I know now that your staying at home to-day to take Sally to the confirmation was just an excuse. You did not want to come with me to Fairfield."

"No, I did not; but I honestly did want to go with Sally: she looked so pretty, mother. I've not been at a confirmation since I was confirmed myself."

"I don't want to talk of that just now, May. Lady Bland is terribly hurt at the way you have treated Cecil. He's quite ill, poor fellow!"

"I'm sorry."

"You are not," snapped Mrs. Webster, "or you would have been kinder to him!"

"Need we go over this oft-trodden ground again?" May asked rather wearily. "I can only reiterate that I really can't and won't marry any one I do not care for."

"I don't believe there is the man in creation that you will care for. It really would be wise for you to accept the one you least dislike."

"Or not marry anybody."

"That is a more than likely alternative. You are five-and-twenty now, and you might have been married over and over again."

May laughed. "I don't know why you are so keen to get rid of me. You will be dreadfully lonely without me; not to say dull."

"That's true enough," said Mrs. Webster, softening; "but a girl like you ought to marry. You won't make a good old maid."

"No," May admitted candidly.

And this question of marriage, which was sorely perplexing

the mistress, was pressing hard also upon her maid, for pretty Rose Lancaster, who had successfully played off her rival suitors against each other for a year, was at last compelled to make her choice between them. Tom Burney had that day received an offer from the squire of a free passage to Tasmania, and a very good appointment on a farm there with a relation of Mr. Lessing's, where, if he gave satisfaction, he might in a few years look forward to part-ownership.

"I only propose to part with you because agriculture does not pay, or I have not learned the way to make it do so," the squire had said. "I have been making up my mind to reduce my staff; and, my cousin having lately written to me about a suitable man, it occurred to me to give you the first offer."

Tom coloured with pleasure. "Thank you, sir; it seems a great chance. It would be a certainty, wouldn't it? I could take another with me."

"Well, it would be wiser for the other fellow to get a promise of work. I might ask if there were an opening," Paul had replied.

"It's not a man as I was thinking of, sir. It was a wife!"

"Oh, I beg your pardon," the squire said laughing. "But if you care for my opinion on a subject of which I know but little, I believe quite the wisest thing you could do would be to take out a wife with you. She would make a home for you and keep you steady. I expect you have some girl in your eye, Burney."

Tom smiled rather sheepishly; it would be time enough to mention Rose when his banns were put up.

And that very afternoon when work was over, Tom had gone

H. Louisa Bedford

home and put on his best clothes; then walked boldly up to the Court and demanded an interview with Rose. She came into the servant's hall where he waited nervously by the fire, and, giving him a careless nod, seated herself and put her toes upon the fender.

"What is it, Tom? I can't stop long; I'm expecting Miss Webster in every minute."

"It's come at last: what I've waited for," stammered Tom. "I've a chance of giving you a home, Rose: a nice one, as far as I can make out."

"Where?" asked Rose, with shining eyes and parted lips, a vision of herself as a bride, in a white frock, and handsome Tom as her bridegroom, floating before her.

"In Tasmania; if you love me well enough to come with me out there. It's a wonderful offer that the squire has given me; and some day I may bring you home almost like a lady."

"But I don't know where it is, and I wouldn't go if I did—not with you nor any man! What can you be thinking of to stuff me up with nonsense like that?" Rose asked poutingly. "I'll have a home on this side of the water, or nowhere."

"And you shall," Tom declared passionately, "if you'll promise to wait until I can make you one!—but I'll have your word for it. You shall have done with Dixon and stick fast by me, or—"

"Or what?" Rose said with rather frightened eyes.

"Or I'll go where you won't be troubled by me any more. Look here! you've held me on for eighteen months now, and, if you cared for me one-half as I love you, you would be ready enough to come with me to the other side of the world, when I can make you an honest offer of a home. I'd follow you to the world's end; ill or well, rich or poor I'd love you just the same; you should not have a trouble that I could keep from you. I've told you so before, and I tell you so to-night; but it's the last time. You can take me or leave me; but I'll know now which it is to be. It don't matter much to me where you want to live, except that, if I don't take this offer, we must wait a bit; but I'll know your mind about it. It must be 'yes' or 'no' to-night!"

Happily for Rose, Miss Webster's bell pealed a noisy summons at that moment.

"I can't stop, Tom! I *really* can't! Miss Webster is not one who can wait. I'll think it over and tell you sometime soon."

"When?" asked Tom, catching her hands and holding them so tightly that she gave a little cry.

"Sunday. Sunday night after church; you can see me home if you like," and with that promise Tom had to be content.

"Mind what you are up to, Rose. Don't play with me too far," he said.

And as Rose sat stitching in the housekeeper's room that night, her mind busied itself over Tom's words, and the difficulty of making a decision. It had never entered Rose's pretty head to lay this question of marriage before God. Had she done so she would have been saved from making a mistake, which was to leave its mark upon the whole of her future life. Her heart drew her one way, and her ambition another. Undoubtedly Tom, with his warm heart and openly expressed devotion, was the man she loved the best of the many who had paid her attention; but she might have to wait for him for years, whilst, if Dixon chose to offer it, he could give her a home to-morrow that any girl in the village might envy; but he had never spoken out as Tom had spoken to-night. His wooing had not been so manly and so straight as poor Tom's. Rose had almost made up her mind to tell him on Sunday that she would wait for him, when a voice waked her from her reverie; and the voice was Dixon's.

"I suppose you don't happen to know if the carriage will be wanted to take the ladies to the station to-morrow? I heard some talk about their going out, but I haven't had any orders."

"I'm not the one to ask! you'll find Mr. Wheeler in the pantry," said Rose, a little sharply.

"What's put you out to-night, I wonder?" said Dixon, coming a little further into the room and closing the door behind him. "Had some quarrel with that peppery lad Burney, I expect? Anyway you've been crying about something; and ten to one it's Burney. I saw him coming away from here, and I had the biggest mind to ask him what business he had to be prowling round a place where he was turned off for unsteadiness."

"You'd best mind what you say about him!" Rose said, stitching away with feverish rapidity. "He wants me to marry him."

"Does he now? Banns put up on Sunday, I suppose?" said Dixon, with a palpable sneer.

"No; we should wait," faltered Rose.

"I should not have thought you were of the waiting sort. Then it's good-bye to me."

"It will be good-bye if I promise; he'll be all or nothing. He's just mad about me."

"Then you've not promised yet?" asked Dixon, eagerly. "You've not been silly enough to do that, Rose?"

"He won't wait; I'm to tell him on Sunday night. And oh! I'm miserable: I don't know what to do!" And Rose let her work fall in her lap, and burst into sobbing.

"Don't cry! don't take on! I'll tell you what to do, my dear. Promise to marry me instead of that hot-headed fool, Burney. Settle it all right away, and don't fash your head any more about it. There need be no waiting—I'll go and see the vicar about the banns,—and if so be that we can't get the rooms over the stables to ourselves, I'll ask Mr. Lessing to give us a cottage. There! you see I'm in earnest. It would be grand to hear your name given out in church the next Sunday as ever is, now wouldn't it?" and Dixon pulled away Rose's hands from her face, and smiled down on her.

"Oh, I couldn't!" Rose said. "There's Tom."

"That would settle Tom fast enough."

Rose never knew quite how it happened; but half an hour later Dixon left without any order for the carriage on the morrow, but with Rose's promise that she would marry him as soon as he liked, and with her consent that the banns should be published on the following Sunday. Rose's silly little head was in such a whirl of delightful excitement that, for the time being, Tom and his misery were forgotten. There was the wedding to think of, and the clothes that must be made, and the question of hat versus veil, for the wedding-day loomed large in the foreground. She wondered how Miss Webster would look when she gave her a month's notice that

H. Louisa Bedford

night; and whether Mrs. Webster would offer to have the wedding breakfast at the Court. It was almost certain that as Dixon was coachman, he would have the loan of the carriage; and she would be driven to the church that day for all the world just like a lady, and half the village would turn out to see her married. And then Tom's large, reproachful eyes, with their expression of dumb pain, stared at her out of the brilliant picture which her imagination conjured. Poor Tom! how would he bear it? She comforted herself a little with the thought that he would be quite certain now to accept the offer of that situation abroad of which he had spoken, and she would not be vexed by the sight of his unhappiness.

"I must not let him meet me on Sunday night. I must write and tell him that Dixon and I have settled it, and that he must not mind too much," thought Rose.

The letter was not an easy one to write, and Rose shelved it. She had a way of shelving unpleasant subjects; but when Saturday night came she could put it off no longer, so, fetching down her writing-case, she spoiled a dozen sheets of paper in the effort to make her news fairly palatable, finally dashing off an unsatisfactory scrawl, badly written and lamely expressed; and, having folded and directed it, she flew out into the yard to find a messenger to take it. The first who presented himself was the groom.

"It would be doing me a real favour if you would let Burney have this note to-night," she said. "It's very particular;" and with the note she shoved sixpence into the man's hand.

He laughed as he pocketed the coin, and was laughing still when he went back into the saddle-room, where Dixon sat smoking over the fire.

"What's the joke, mate?"

"A note from your girl to Burney—'very particular' she called it! I'll warrant it's to tell him he'd better not come this way any more."

"I dare say it is," replied Dixon, slowly. "Hand it over; I'm going down to the village, and I'll leave it myself."

The groom hesitated. "I think I'll stick to it; she gave me sixpence to make sure he got it, and I wouldn't like to cheat her."

"Stick to the sixpence but give me the letter. Who's a better right to it than I, I should like to know? I'm as good as married already," said Dixon, stretching out his hand.

"You'll promise not to forget."

"I'm not one as forgets," said Dixon, with an odd laugh.

"And if there's any mistake you'll settle it?"

"Yes; I'll settle it."

The groom gave the note and went out whistling; he was not quite easy in his mind about the missive. Left to himself, Dixon turned the envelope round in his fingers, examining it back and front. The blotted writing gave evidence of hurry, the blistered paper testified to tears, and Dixon broke into an oath.

"The little jade!—that's the second time she's cried about him this week to my certain knowledge," he said aloud. "She would not dare to chuck me now, though, even if she does love the other one; but I've more than half a mind to put this in the fire. It may be to tell him that she's settled things with me; but it would not be a bad joke to let him hear it for himself in church, and her telling him nothing about it, good or bad, would let him know she did not care much for him."

In another moment there was a brief blaze in the fire, and Rose's note was reduced to ashes.

The next morning Tom Burney rose with the feeling that he trod on air, such a strange exhilaration of spirit possessed him.

He had heard nothing from Rose during the week, and her very silence filled him with hope. If she meant to refuse him, he was almost sure that she would have put him out of his misery before this. He was not generally a vain fellow, but to-day his toilet was a matter of moment; his tie was re-adjusted half a dozen times, and he asked his landlady to give him a chrysanthemum for his buttonhole.

"Goin' courtin'?" she said, with a laugh as she pinned it in for him. And Tom coloured rosy red, but said nothing.

He started early for church, hoping that he might catch a glimpse of Rose as she passed in with the other servants from the Court; but either she had got there before him, or, for some unknown cause, she had been detained at home. Dixon presently appeared, smart and neat, giving Tom an affable nod as he passed up the path to the church; but Tom's eyes were fixed straight in front of him, and he ignored the greeting.

"I'll not pretend to be friends when I ain't," he said to himself.

Presently the hurrying bell warned the outside group of stragglers to make their way into church; and Tom took his usual seat at the end of the nave. It is to be feared that his thoughts that morning were not occupied with devotion. Prayer and psalm passed unheeded over his head; but when, at the end of the second lesson, there was a pause, and the rector turned over the leaves of a book in front of him, Tom lifted his head and waited for the banns that would follow. Before long he might be listening to the publishing of his own.

"I publish the banns of marriage between William Dixon, bachelor, and Rose Lancaster, spinster, both of this parish...."

Was it some ghastly nightmare, Tom wondered, as he clutched at the seat in front of him? But the suppressed grin on the faces near him, the foolish smile with which the publishing of banns is so often received in a village church, convinced him that he had heard aright. The blood was rioting to his brain, and the beating in his throat made him put up his hand with the vain endeavour to loosen his collar lest he should choke there and then with the passion that could find no outlet. For one instant he was possessed by a wild wish to stand up and forbid the banns; but what end would be gained by making himself a greater laughing-stock to the village than he was at present, for already he felt the derisive finger of scorn pointed at him as the man whom Rose had jilted. Even now he saw one or two of the lads nudge each other and look at him with curious eyes. To be watched at such a moment was torture, and, like an animal in pain, Tom longed for solitude. He groped blindly under the seat for his hat, made his way to the door and slipped out. He stumbled on like a man in delirium, looking neither to the right nor left, but following instinctively the path across the fields which led to the river. The turbulence of its grey waters, as it rushed on to the sea, seemed most in keeping with the wild, wicked thoughts that surged unchecked through his brain, and were bearing him he knew not whither. He threw himself upon the long, rank grass on the bank, still wet with the heavy mist of night, and, pillowing his chin in his hands, watched with dilating eyes the swirling river as it swept by. A giddiness dimmed his vision, a singing filled his ears.

"If I slipped over and was carried along with it, there'd be an end of it all," thought Tom. And the chill wind came sighing across the water, and shook the heavy rushes at the edge, which seemed whisperingly to echo his thought, "an end of it all."

Then Tom half-angrily roused himself, and pressed his hands to the eyes that burned like fire, and tried to collect his bewildered senses. What!—slip out of life like a drowned rat and never see Rose again, nor tell her what he knew of the man she had chosen in preference to him. She would be glad to know he was dead, he told himself with fierce bitterness. She had played with him like a cat with a mouse for more than a year but in the long run the mouse died squeaking. Surely she could not be so false-hearted as to break faith with him to-night; she would meet him and say good-bye? She *should* meet him, whether she liked it or not; and if Dixon were with her so much the better,—and Tom's fists clenched involuntarily.

For hours and hours he wandered, following the windings of the river, until, as the November sun paled and sank in a bank of grey cloud, he discovered that he was some six or eight miles from Rudham, and that his knees were knocking together with mingled emotion and fatigue. A wayside inn seemed a haven of refuge to him in his exhausted condition. Through the red blind of the bar a light shone cheerily, and Tom entered the door without knocking, and, seating himself on the settle by the fire, ordered sixpennyworth of brandy.

"Hot water or cold? You'll have it hot, if you take my advice," said the landlady, with a glance at the bloodshot eyes that glared so strangely out of the deathly white face.

"Neither, thanks," said Tom, tossing off the raw spirit at a gulp.

It tasted to him like so much water; it did not muddle his brain, it cleared it, it nerved him for that interview with Rose.

"Another sixpennyworth, please," he said, laying down a shilling on the table.

The landlady paused, and coughed behind her hand; she had sons of her own.

"I wouldn't if I was you," she said, pushing him back sixpence. "You've took as much as is good for you, and ne'er a drop of water.

"You can serve me or leave it alone," said Tom, angrily. "I'm ill; I need it. It tastes like so much water."

The landlady shook her head but gave him the brandy, and Tom, having swallowed it, bade her a civil good night and went on his way.

The landlady hurried to the door and looked after him; he was walking very fast but quite straight.

"It may have gone to his head, but it's not got into his legs," she said, a note of admiration in her voice.

Tom meanwhile hurried on to the station, which he knew to be not more than half a mile away. He was just in time to

H. Louisa Bedford

catch the one down-train that ran on Sunday evening, which would land him in Rudham in time for evening service—not that Tom meant to go to church that night. He would walk outside and wait for Dixon and for Rose. Many a time the two men had escorted Rose back to the Court, one on either side. This would be the last.

CHAPTER XI

A FRIEND IN NEED

Rose Lancaster had never looked prettier than that Sunday night, as she tripped into church, a soft ruffle of fur setting off the delicate fair face, a large velvet hat resting on the golden hair. Dixon, with a proud air of possession, walked in behind her, and, seating himself at her side, proved his proprietorship by producing her Prayer-book from his pocket, and finding all her places for her throughout the service. When Rose dared to lift her head and look about her, she gave a sigh of relief to see that Tom was not present.

"I dare say he thought I should like it best if he stayed away," she thought. She was thankful that the question of her marriage was decided and well decided.

The moon had risen when the service ended. There was a group of people collected outside the church-gate discussing the village gossip before they dispersed to their several homes.

Dixon pulled Rose's arm through his own, and, not allowing her to linger for a moment, led her off. They did not either of them notice that a man with a hat well pulled over his eyes followed them at some little distance; and not until the

H. Louisa Bedford

village was left behind, and the pair had turned into the road, which, with many a wind, led up to the Court, did he attempt to lessen the space which separated them. Then, as unconsciously Rose and Dixon walked more slowly, Tom quickened his steps, and was alongside of them before they realized his presence. He pushed back his hat; and Rose broke into a smothered cry of alarm as the moonlight fell upon the haggard face and wild eyes of her rejected lover, and she clung the tighter to Dixon's arm.

Tom's laugh was not pleasant to listen to. "You asked for my company, Rose, but you don't seem best pleased now I've come," he said; "but, pleased or not, I'll walk with you to-night, and say a thing or two it's right for you to hear before we part company for good."

"I wrote to you," stammered Rose. "I sent it by a special messenger on Saturday night to tell you that, after thinking things over, I'd—I'd—"

"She made up her mind that I should be the best husband for her," said Dixon, putting a protecting arm round Rose's shoulder, and finishing off the sentence she found it so difficult to frame.

The words and the action alike maddened Tom. Was Rose to be protected from him when, to give her pleasure and shield her from pain, had been his one thought for the last eighteen months?

"It's only fair that, as she's chucked me for you, she should know the sort of man she's got hold of," he stuttered.

"I didn't lose my place for being so drunk that it took the parson the best part of the night to see me home, did I?" sneered Dixon.

"No, you didn't. But Rose shall hear now who plotted to make me drunk that night, and who informed against me next day. It was you, you sly, sneaking scamp!—deny it if you dare? If it comes to character who's got the better one, you or I? No man can throw a dirty, dishonest trick at me! And you! Who squares the corn-merchant? Who cooks every bill that goes into the Court? Don't I know it? Have I lived nearly a year under the same roof that covered you, without finding out pretty well how you've managed to feather your nest so as to make it fine enough for the pretty bird you've caught; and if I'd chosen to round on you when you got me turned out, where would you be now, I'd like to know? You would not be coachman at the Court."

Dixon had turned livid with rage, but kept his head.

"You are a poor, drunken fool, and don't know what you are saying, or I'd make you swallow your words."

"You wouldn't! I could prove them!" went on Tom, choking with passion. "And as you've cheated in work, you've cheated in love. You've cheated me, and you've cheated that one as followed you sobbing and crying from the place where you last came from, and who you'd promised faithful to marry, and who you'd walked with for three years and more. I had the story from the woman where I lodge. The girl spent the night there, and she was pretty nigh broken-hearted. She'd even got her wedding-gown."

Dixon sprang across the road like a tiger, and gave Tom such a swinging box on the ear that, for a moment, he reeled again. And then, all the devil in Tom was loosed, and he leaped on his foe, gripping him by the throat until every vein in his forehead stood out in blue knots. The action was so unexpected and so rapid that Dixon found it impossible to free himself. The men swayed to and fro in each other's embrace, finally falling heavily together with a sickening thud upon the road. Tom was uppermost, and picked himself up with a rather ghastly smile, but Dixon lay there rigid and motionless.

"Get up!" said Tom, poking him with the toe of his boot. "You won't be so ready to interfere with me another time." But Dixon did not stir.

Rose, who had tried to stop the quarrel by every artifice in her power, knelt down by the side of her lover. And suddenly a cry so shrill, so despairing, broke the air, that Tom's heart stood still and the blood froze in his veins.

"Tom! Tom!—you wicked man, you've killed him!" she shrieked.

And Tom, sobered by the cry, and realizing in all its horror the meaning of the words, turned like guilty Cain and fled. There was but one place for him now: the river—the river, and the end of it all. He was making for it straight, flying by the nearest cut across the fields, leaping ditches, scrambling through hedges, regardless of the brambles that scored his face and hands. Like a hare hunted by the hounds he fled; away from his own guilty action, away from the woman he loved, to the river which would sweep him swiftly, painlessly to rest and forgetfulness. But would it? He had stumbled accidentally into the path which led towards the cottage where he lodged, and turned his head as he ran to take one last glance at the light which glimmered in the window. He could see the river now; he was nearing the brink. There was but one field between him and it, when he became conscious of a pursuing step. Somebody was already on his scent. The question now was whether he should die by his own act, or be delivered over to the terrible hands of justice; and at that thought Tom redoubled his speed to outstrip his pursuer. It was a desperate race, for his strength was nearly spent. His long fast had told upon him, and the fictitious power of the spirit he had swallowed had passed away. His breath was coming in quick, short gasps. His foot caught in a tussock of grass, and he fell face foremost to the ground, and, before he could regain his feet, a hand was on his collar.

"Let me go! Let me go!" he cried, struggling desperately in the hands of his capturer. "If I've killed him I'm ready to die too. You can't do more than hang me! One more moment and I'd have been in the river. Let me go, I say!"

"I shall *not* let you go; you are either mad or drunk—incapable of taking care of yourself," said a low, clear voice; and Tom was lifted to a standing posture by the rector's strong arms.

* * * * * *

When Dixon had called late on Saturday night to ask the rector to put up his banns on the morrow, Mr. Curzon's thoughts flew straight to Tom. So this was the end of his love-story, poor fellow! and he feared that it would go hardly with the lad.

"Maybe he will come to see me to-morrow. And, if not, I will see him," he had said.

He had noticed with satisfaction that Tom was in his accustomed place on Sunday morning, and did not see him slip out of church after the publishing of the banns; but on Sunday night he missed him, and, the minute service was ended, he set off for the cottage where he lodged. He had reached the field-path which led to it, when he heard the sound of footsteps that stumbled in their running, and,

H. Louisa Bedford

pausing to look round, he saw a figure, which he did not immediately recognize in the moonlight as Tom's, dashing across the pathway in the direction of the river. Almost before he knew what he was doing the rector gave chase, for he felt the man meant mischief: a conviction which grew into certainty as he gained upon the runaway, and recognized him as the man whom he sought.

Tom attempted no further resistance, and, from his incoherent utterances, Mr. Curzon presently gathered what had occurred.

"And you ran off and left Rose with her dead lover? I could not have believed you such a coward, Tom!" he said, unable to keep back the indignation and scorn he felt. "This is no place for you and me; we must go back at once, and see if anything can be done."

Nothing was said as the two hastened back to the spot where Dixon was left lying; but, to the utter astonishment of both, when they arrived there, Rose and Dixon had gone.

"Either some vehicle has driven by which has conveyed Dixon to the Court, or he was, by God's mercy, only stunned," said the rector. "We'll go on and find out."

Tom made no answer, but followed the rector's lead. In a kind of dumb despair he felt he was walking to meet his fate. They made their way first to the stables, anxious not to give the alarm at the house until they knew the extent of the mischief. The usual orderly quiet prevailed, and, in response to the rector's knock, the groom, who had played such a faithless part by Rose, appeared.

"Is Dixon in? Can I see him for a moment?" asked Mr. Curzon, guardedly.

"He came in, sir, about a quarter of an hour since, but he's gone straight up to bed. He'd a nasty fall—did not know quite how he'd done it, slipped up on his heel, he said, and fell on the back of his head. Rose Lancaster was with him, and seemed terrible cut up about it, said he lay like a dead thing; and she would never have got him home if it had not been that a cart drove by and gave 'em both a lift."

"Thank you. Tell Dixon that I'll come round in the morning to see how he is."

"We need do nothing more to-night; your worst fear is not realized," he said, as he and Tom turned towards home. "Now you will come back to supper with me, and we will trace your sin to its very root, please God. You've had a warning that I think you are not likely to forget."

But Tom, in the sudden relief from the horrible fear that he had inadvertently taken the life of a fellow creature, had broken into a passion of sobs, shedding such tears as a man sheds but once in a lifetime—scalding tears of bitter repentance and shame.

He and Mr. Curzon sat talking far into the night, and Tom told the story truly, keeping nothing back.

"You've let drink and passion get the upper hand, Tom. You have put the love of a woman before the love of God, and you've come near to wrecking your life and hers in consequence. It would not have mended matters if you had hurried yourself into another world to which you have given so little thought, would it? It was a mad, wicked thought! a thought of the devil's own suggestion; but you are saved for the beginning of a better life, a new life in new surroundings."

H. Louisa Bedford

Tom glanced up quickly. "Not in Tasmania," he said. "The squire won't send me, after this."

"You'll tell him about it, then," replied Mr. Curzon, with a heart-throb of thanksgiving that Tom was ready to face out the consequences of his action.

"Oh yes; I shall tell him. He might hear it any way, but I'd rather tell him myself."

"Very good. Now you had better go home to bed, and, if you have never said a real prayer before, you will say one to-night, Tom, to the God who has saved you from falling over a precipice of crime."

Tom nodded; his heart was too full to speak.

When the morning broke it found the rector in his study where Tom had left him, still upon his knees, for here and there, in this hurrying nineteenth century world, there is yet found a disciple who, like the Master whom he serves, will spend whole nights in prayer. Was not the salvation of a soul at stake?

A fresh development of Rose Lancaster's love-affairs was brought to Mr. Curzon's notice on Monday, for the first person he met, as he left the rectory in the morning, was Rose herself—a crumpled dishevelled Rose, whose toilet gave evidence of hurry, and whose eyes were red with weeping.

"Oh, sir, I've come because I didn't know what to do. We're all in dreadful trouble!—Dixon's gone!"

"Not dead!" cried the rector in horror.

"Oh no; he's run away. And oh, it's cruel, cruel! to have used me like this," said Rose, her sobs bursting out afresh.

"I wonder what has made him do it? Has he left no note behind him?"

"Not a line—nor a message for me," replied Rose. "Only a scrawl in pencil which the groom found on the saddle-room table, to say that nobody need try to trace him. And only to think that our banns were put up yesterday."

"I think you are wasting your tears over a heartless scamp!" said the rector, a little impatiently. "Did you come with any message from the Court?"

"No, sir; I only came to ask you if I ought to tell?"

"To tell what?"

"All that happened last night. There was a dreadful quarrel between Dixon and Tom Burney; and that's how Dixon got hurt. He was stunned, and I thought he was dead; and Tom ran off, and, when Dixon came to himself, his one notion was that I was not to tell any one how he came by his fall."

"So you promised to back him up in a lie!" said the rector, coldly. "One can scarcely wonder that you wished to keep the thing quiet, however. You've terribly misused God's good gift of a pretty face, Rose. You have played with two men; and chosen the wrong one, and driven the other half off his head with misery. Mercifully the good God has saved you from what must have been a miserable marriage, for there is more in Dixon's disappearance than we can see just yet."

Rose's tears dried with her gathering indignation. It had not occurred to her to blame herself in any way; she felt rather in

H. Louisa Bedford

the position of the ill-used heroine of a tragedy in real life.

"Then you think I ought to tell," she said a little sulkily.

"I certainly think your mistress ought to know exactly what happened. You need not tell any one else, that I know of."

So Rose returned to the Court greatly crestfallen; and her account of the quarrel, and Tom's vague threats about Dixon's character, put Mrs. Webster on to the right clue as to the causes of his sudden flight. He was found to have been guilty of repeated acts of dishonesty, so cleverly concealed that, but for the fear that Tom would report him, he might have gone on for years longer, respected and trusted by his employers. As the time seemed ripe for flight, however, he had taken with him the change of a big cheque that Mrs. Webster had given him to cash on the Saturday, and which he had told her glibly that he could not get cashed until the Monday. Each fresh revelation filled Rose with misery and shame; and, behind all, was the one fact that she had kept to herself: the memory of Tom's mention of that other girl that Dixon had jilted—the crowning taunt which had hurried Dixon into showing fight.

"And it must have been true, or it would not have made him so angry," thought Rose.

It was a bitter pill for the vain little thing to swallow: the conviction that she had all along occupied the second place in Dixon's affections, and that he had cast her away, like that other girl, without any compunction. Tom would not have done it; and at the remembrance of him Rose's eyes filled with tears. Rose was returning from the village, whither she had been sent on a message, and she shivered a little as she passed the scene of the last night's disaster; and her alarm found expression in a little cry when she saw Tom Burney standing there, too, and yet there was nothing to terrify her in the deprecating glance of his troubled eyes.

"Rose," he said, stretching out his hands, "I don't wonder that you hate the sight of me, but you can afford to speak kindly to me for this once? God knows I'm sorry enough for what I've done, heart sorry. I came here to look at the place again, where I nearly killed a man, just to let it burn in so that I mayn't forget."

"But—but—you can't have heard that he's not much hurt even? that he's run away and taken a lot of money that does not belong to him?"

"Oh yes," said Tom, drearily. "But that does not alter things; I can't forget that I nearly killed him—and myself."

"Oh, Tom, not that! not that!" cried Rose, for the first time pierced by a pang of keen remorse.

"Yes. I should have drowned myself if Mr. Curzon had not stopped me," said Tom, simply. "I was mad, I think, with misery and drink."

Then Rose understood the full meaning of the rector's words that morning.

"I did not mean to try and see you before I went away," went on Tom, brokenly; "but I'm glad of the chance to ask your forgiveness for the hurt I might have done to the man you wished to marry."

"Oh don't! please don't talk like that!" said Rose, Tom's utter self-abasement and humility rousing all her better nature. "Don't you see that it's you who ought to forgive me for the cruel way I've treated you; and if you'd died, Tom, and my

H. Louisa Bedford

wickedness had killed you, how could I have ever lifted up my head again? I see now how wicked I've been. I wanted to marry Dixon because he promised to give me everything I liked: a pretty house and a little servant, and pretty clothes and things. It was not because I loved him best."

Tom threw back his head with a little cry.

"Rose," he said, coming a step nearer. "Rose, my dear; it can't hurt to tell me now. In two days I'm going away for good and all. I have told the squire all about it, and he is going to overlook it and send me across the seas just the same as if nothing had happened; but when I'm gone, it would make me happy to know that you had ever loved me just a little bit."

"I do," said Rose. "I think I've loved you all the time."

Tom drew a long breath, but did not attempt to come closer.

"Thank you," he said, with an odd thrill in his voice. "I'll go away and think of it. It will help me to be good, for I'll have a try at that, Rose, my dear. I'll keep clear of the drink; I'm going up to the rector to-night to tell him I'm ready to sign. He asked me to do it before; and don't I wish I had listened to him! But now I'll do it without the asking."

There was some difference in Tom that Rose felt but could not define, some influence over him that was stronger than her own. She had been conscious before that she had but to speak and he would try his utmost to carry out her whim; but to-day, miserable as he was, oppressed by the weight of sin, she felt respect for a certain strength of purpose that seemed developed in him. Mr. Curzon was right; she had chosen the wrong man. Never had she valued Tom's love as she did now when she was just about to lose it.

"Then you are going directly?" she almost whispered.

"Yes; I leave here the day after to-morrow, and I sail in about a fortnight. The squire thought the sooner I was out of the way the better."

"Shall you ever come back?"

"I don't know."

"Nor ever write?" asked Rose, with a sob in her throat.

"That's as may be; I'd write to one who cared."

"I care. Write to me, please?"

She was looking at him with pleading eyes, but he would not trust himself to return her glance.

"Rose," he said, "there's not the woman now that I would ask to be my wife. I'm guilty, before God, of two black sins; but if He gives me time to live it down and earn a clean name again—"

"He will! He will!" said Rose. "And, Tom, it does not matter if it's years, I'll wait." And then she put her arms round his neck and kissed him.

His face was ashen grey; his arms ached with the longing to return her embrace and hold her close to his heart, but he let her go.

"Before God, Rose, my darling, I'll live worthy of your kiss! Maybe it won't be long before I dare return it."

The next instant he was gone, not daring to look back at her.

H. Louisa Bedford

CHAPTER XII

KITTY'S CHRISTMAS TREE

"The Websters are off to London, Paul," said Sally, about two days after Tom's departure.

Paul started at the sudden mention of the name.

"I did not think they intended to go to town until after the New Year. Mrs. Webster dilates largely upon the superiority of a Christmas in the country versus a Christmas in London; but, I suppose, it is as sincere as most of her statements?"

"I think May has had more to do with it than her mother. She says Mrs. Webster has fussed a good deal over Dixon's flight, she trusted him so thoroughly. And May thinks it will be easier to get a good coachman in London, and that it will take off her mother's thoughts from an unpleasant subject. She now has visions of Dixon's return in company with an armed body of burglars, and prophesies cheerfully that they will all be found dead in their beds one morning, and that the house will be ransacked."

Paul laughed. "Under the circumstances Miss Webster is wise to remove her forcibly to London," he said. But he privately conjectured that May's real reason for flight lay in her desire to get away from himself. "Has anything been heard of Dixon?" he went on.

"Nothing. I don't think any very keen search has been made for him. Mrs. Webster declares that she would far rather lose her money than appear in a court of law, or have her name bandied about in the papers. I think, Paul, that if you approve I shall be off to London, too, when the New Year comes."

"In what capacity?" asked Paul, resignedly. "As a sister or something?"

"Oh dear, no; you know I've always wanted to join one of those settlements of girls at the East End, who work under the management of Miss Grant. She wrote a little while ago to tell me she would have a vacancy in the settlement soon after Christmas. My work would lie chiefly amongst factory girls, getting up statistics about their hours of work and their housing, and my play would be recreation evenings with them."

"But this is what you have always talked of doing. I expected you to take up quite different lines now: to district visit, and take classes on Sundays, under the guidance and supervision of the rector."

"I don't feel the least fitted for it; I know very little about it. Mr. Curzon thinks it would be a great pity for me to abandon the work to which I feel myself drawn. I like life in London far better than in the country."

"I quite agree with you," interposed Paul.

"And I think that my change of opinion about religious things will help, rather than hinder me in my work," continued Sally, with a slight effort.

H. Louisa Bedford

"Let us hope it may," said Paul, in a tone that implied a doubt on the subject. "Anyway, I wish you to follow your own plan of life. I think women ought to be as free as men to choose what they will do. But"—with a glance from the window—"Miss Kitty's carriage stops the way. I must go and see what she wants."

"Why, Kitty," he began, almost before he had reached the gate, "I thought you had forgotten all about me! It is days, almost weeks, I think, since you've paid me a call."

"It's because it has rained nearly every day and I've not been out at all; and there are such a lot of things I want to ask you about."

Paul was Kitty's referee on every subject. "What is the first, I wonder?" he said, smiling down at her.

"Bend down, please, Mr. Paul. It's a secret."

And Paul brought his ear to a level with Kitty's mouth.

"Do boys like Noah's Arks?"

Paul straightened himself with a burst of laughter.

"I thought you would know. Nurse said you'd be sure to know," Kitty said, much injured by his untimely mirth.

"It's just because I don't that I am laughing," said Paul, whose remembrance of childhood was unconnected with any scriptural game. That he should be solemnly consulted about one seemed extremely ludicrous.

"Then you did not have one?"

"No, I did not."

"I suppose it won't do, after all," said Kitty, dejectedly. "And it's a real beauty; it cost half a crown."

"Really! That's a big price. I should think it might do for any one. After all, an ark might come in handy soon, if we are going to have a flood. Who's the happy boy?"

"Oh, you are shouting!" cried Kitty, warningly. "And it's a secret."

"I beg your pardon," said Paul, penitently. "Shall I look in and give an opinion?"

"Yes; you and Sally, too. Perhaps you would come to tea with me this afternoon? Daddy is gone to a Congress, or he could have told me everything."

"Yes, we will come—Sally and I."

"And then I can tell you all about it, for Nurse knows but has promised not to tell."

"We will try to be as trustworthy as Nurse," Paul said with a reassuring nod.

So, over tea and toast, after three false guesses on Paul and Sally's part, Kitty divulged her tremendous secret, which turned out to be that daddy had promised that when she was ten years old she should give a Christmas-tree party to every child in Rudham from ten years and under, and the whole responsibility of choosing the presents and assorting them should devolve upon her. For months past Kitty had been making out her list of the children she would have to invite, rather bewildering the villagers by her feverish anxiety to

H. Louisa Bedford

discover the ages of their offspring; but the choosing of suitable presents for her guests was a far more difficult task. A large box of toys had arrived, by her father's order, from a neighbouring town, from which Kitty could make a selection; she had spent one whole day poring over them. Girls were easy enough to please, but boys' tastes were quite a different matter. So Nurse had finally suggested that Mr. Lessing should be taken into confidence. Happily, by the afternoon he had grasped the gravity of the situation, and he discussed the varying merits of tops, marbles, horses, and carts as earnestly as even Kitty could desire. He still felt a lurking desire to laugh when he saw the Noah's Ark, which cost half a crown, set apart in a place by itself on Kitty's couch. From time to time she laid a caressing hand upon it. It was still unallotted, and Kitty gave a quivering sigh of excitement as she glanced down her crumpled list.

"I had meant this for Tommy Baird," she said, looking down at it fondly. "It's quite the best thing I have—and he's the oldest boy,—and it's very pretty, daddy thinks; but you say it won't do."

"I!" cried Paul, aghast. "I never said anything of the kind."

"You laughed at it! and you said something about a flood."

"Was not the ark connected with a flood? You know better than I."

Kitty looked from Paul to Sally with distress on her face.

"Of course," she said, a little petulantly. "But you said there might be another—and there can't be, daddy says."

"Of course there can't," said Paul, a little hurriedly, feeling it scarcely fair to make a joke to such a sensitive little girl.

"Look here! I'm writing a ticket for Tommy Baird, and I shall tuck it under the elephant's trunk. Do you think he will hold it fast?"

"Then it will do, after all," said Kitty, greatly relieved.

But when Paul and Sally were gone, and all the excitement and joy of the tea-party, and the allotting of her presents, was over, Kitty's mind reverted to the flood. Mr. Paul had meant something which he would not explain to her. Whilst the perplexing thought was still in her mind, she heard her father's latchkey turn in the lock of the front door, and he popped his head into the room where she lay with a merry laugh.

"I'm home, Kitty. I'll be down in a minute, but I must get my things off first. It is raining cats and dogs."

The words confirmed Kitty's worst fears. That is how it must have rained before that first great flood, when the waters crept up and up, and the people first climbed the hills, until the waters reached them there; and at last there was nothing to be seen anywhere but a waste of water and one little ark that floated on the top. By the time Mr. Curzon came and seated himself by her side, Kitty's eyes were round with the terror of the picture that her too vivid imagination had painted. Her father, quick to read each passing emotion on the face that was dearest to him in the whole world, stooped down and kissed her.

"My little Kitty is in one of her frightened moods. She must tell me all about it."

"It's the flood," Kitty whispered.

"What flood, darling?"

H. Louisa Bedford

"Mr. Paul said we might have one."

"Did he? He must have meant that the river might overflow its banks; and perhaps it will after such a wet season."

"But it would drown us all."

"Not a bit of it. The cottages near the river might have some water in them; but unless it were something quite unprecedented, the water would not get to the upper floor of any house—and certainly won't come near us or the church and schools, so you may dismiss your fear of a flood. You ought not to have had it anyway, because God has promised that the world shall not be flooded totally again. Shall I tell you what a very good man wrote years ago—many hundreds of years ago—about floods? 'The floods are risen, O Lord, the floods have lift up their voice, the floods lift up their waves... but yet the Lord who dwelleth on high, is mightier.' If he could learn that, all that long time ago, you ought not to be afraid now, ought you?"

"And you don't think God will let it come before my Christmas tree, do you daddy? Because, if all the little children were obliged to stay upstairs, to keep out of the way of the water, they could not come," said Kitty, giving a strictly practical turn to the conversation.

Mr. Curzon smiled and stroked Kitty's head.

"That is more than I can say, darling. Although your Christmas tree seems such a big thing to you, it is only a little one; and if it were put off it would be a disappointment to you, but not a trouble, you see."

Kitty was silenced but not satisfied, and each night added a postscript to her prayers that the flood, if it was to come, should not occur before her Christmas tree. It was to be held in the school-room on Christmas Eve. The secret had exploded now, for the invitations were out, each one written by Kitty herself, and personally delivered in the course of her morning rambles. Paul and Sally were to come as humble helpers. December 23rd was a particularly wild, wet day; but a gleam of sunshine at the close of it produced a rainbow so brilliant in hue that Kitty regarded it as a written sign in the heavens that the flood would be averted, certainly until after her Christmas tree. But it was such a brief gleam of sun! All night through the rain fell, and the wind, which had been fairly quiet the previous day, rose to a perfect tempest, roaring in the tree-tops round the rectory, groaning in the chimneys, and dashing the rain in sheets against poor little Kitty's window-pane; and when in the morning Nurse drew up the blind, and burst into an exclamation of surprise, Kitty knew that her worst fear was realized, and that her prayer had been unavailing. The "Lord that dwelt on high" did not seem to have listened. She tried to nerve herself to bear the tidings which Nurse conveyed in as cheerful a tone as she could assume.

"Miss Kitty, my dear, what do you think has happened? The waters are out, and the river is turned into a great big lake, and the houses are standing out of it like little dots. It all looks so funny; shall I lift you out to see?"

But Kitty had buried her head under the clothes, and was sobbing quietly to herself. No mention was made of the Christmas tree in her prayers that morning, and the prayers themselves were very perfunctory indeed—said more from the force of habit than because she had any faith in their efficacy. True, the rain had ceased now, but what was the good of that now the flood had come? And the worst of it was that she could not talk this matter out to daddy; he would think her dreadfully wicked. So it was a very white-faced Kitty that presented herself at the breakfast-table, and she received her father's assurance that her tree should not be abandoned, but only delayed, with a watery, quivering smile.

"And I shall be so busy all the morning," went on Mr. Curzon, cheerfully. "You see, lots of the cottages are cut off from communication with the outside world, and the children will be hungry and wanting their breakfasts and dinners; so I must be off to see what I can do with carts or boats, according to the depth of the water."

This was rather exciting; and Kitty spent her morning with her chair drawn close to the window, which commanded the best view of the village, and saw carts drawn by pairs of horses splashing along to some of the cottages. And to one cottage, standing alone in a low-lying field, she saw a boat making its way; she was almost sure that the man who rowed it was her friend Mr. Paul. Later in the morning he paid her a visit, with a red colour in his face and a cheery ring in his voice.

"I could not get up before, Kitty. We have had such a lot to do, Sally and I, taking round supplies to the people who are flooded. Everybody is in quite good spirits—indeed, some of the children are thinking it first-rate fun."

At the mention of the children Kitty broke down helplessly, and sobbed aloud.

"Dear me! And I have had such a lot of water all the morning, I did not expect a shower-bath here. What time do you expect Sally and me? How long will it take to light up that blessed tree?"

Kitty uncovered one eye; Mr. Paul must be dreaming.

"I can't have it, you see."

"Who said so? Sally and I have been planning all the morning how we shall order out all my waggons, and go round and fetch your guests—only you must not have the tree too late, or else we might lose our way in taking them home again."

Kitty's joy could only find expressions in incoherent exclamations of delight.

"It's wonderfully kind of you," said the rector, who appeared at that moment, and gradually gathered from Kitty what Paul proposed to do.

"It seems a pity the thing should be put off," Paul answered a little awkwardly.

Perhaps no act of the squire's won such universal approbation as the spirited manner in which he carried through Miss Kitty's tree.

"You would not have thought as he was one to care about the little ones," said Mrs. Macdonald to Sally.

"And I don't think, honestly, that he is," Sally answered— "with the exception of Kitty Curzon; his devotion to her is something quite astonishing."

The tree had been, happily, trimmed the day before, and nothing therefore remained but for the guests to appear. One or two had to be fetched in a boat, and the cottage in the field had a special voyage to itself. There was a little child there that was a particular friend of Kitty's.

"It's very good of you to come, sir, but I'm not sure as I can let Jenny go; she's been ailing all day," said the smiling mother, looking out at Paul from an upstairs window. "She's felt the damp a bit. The water's begun to go down already. We'll be able to get downstairs again to-morrow; but, as I was saying to my mate, it will be the queerest Christmas Day we've ever spent."

"Yes, indeed," said Paul, hurriedly, anxious to cut short the disconnected speech; "but I think you must let me have Jenny, Mrs. Weldon. She's such a great friend of Kitty's, and we shall not have any more rain for the present. Put on an extra shawl. It will be fine fun for Jenny to have a ride in a boat."

So Jenny, wrapped up so that only her eyes were visible, was handed out; and Paul rowed her across the field that separated her from dry land, popping her into a cart that waited on the far side.

Sally, meanwhile, was at the school arranging the children as they arrived, whilst Kitty's carriage was drawn up close to the tree, which was veiled under a sheet. Jenny Weldon was the last to arrive, and, when duly uncloaked, was given a place close to Kitty.

Then followed the lighting of the tree; and the dancing eyes of the children watched the process with untold delight. Joining hands they walked round it singing a quaint old Christmas carol, led by the rector's strong sonorous voice; and finally came the distribution of the presents.

Paul, as he stood quietly at the back of the room, thought the scene a pretty one. It was a beautiful tradition, that of the Christ Child; he could have almost wished it true.

"It has come to an end—I think it has really come to an end," the rector said. "But, stay, I find some little things tucked away at the very bottom of the tree; and here upon the labels are written 'Miss Lessing' and 'Mr. Lessing.' That is quite as it should be, for to whom do we owe the fact of your all being here to-night but to the squire, who planned and carried it out?"

And as a penknife was handed to Paul, there were cheers ringing in his ears for him and for Sally, who had a pen with her name on it.

"It was really very jolly of you, Kitty," said Paul, making his way to her.

"Weren't you surprised?" said Kitty, joyfully. "Daddy said you would be; and I told him where to hide them so that Sally should not see them. And, oh!"—with a long-drawn sigh—"I've never been so happy in my life. Daddy says I must thank you ever so much, dear Mr. Paul."

Paul stooped and kissed the pretty, flushed face. "It's been great fun, Kitty; you've nothing to thank me for. It is my first Christmas tree, and I shall take great care of my penknife."

It was seven o'clock before Sally and Paul regained the quietness and peace of their lodging, for it took some time to deliver all the little ones to their several homes.

"It's wonderful what surroundings will do for one. I've felt as if I were a curate to-day; but it is Kitty who drove me to it. Her despair this morning was almost tragic," Paul said.

How little he knew that that night Kitty was thanking God for her happy day, and for the special help He had sent her to

H. Louisa Bedford

carry through her tree.

"Pray bless dear Mr. Paul!"

CHAPTER XIII

THE CALL OF GOD

With the dawn of the New Year there was an outbreak of fever in Rudham, the after-effect of the flood, which, although it subsided almost as quickly as it rose, left the houses which it had invaded damp and many of the drains blocked. Paul, as he went his rounds, condemned some of the cottages as insanitary, and determined that another spring should see new ones begun in higher, healthier situations— if, at least, he could by any means raise the requisite funds. He was constantly brought into contact with the rector, who busied himself amongst his sick people morning, noon, and night.

"Bless you!" said Mrs. Weldon, when Paul had been looking round her premises, and heard with some astonishment the sound of a strong, clear voice singing in the bedroom above, "that's only Mr. Curzon singing hymns to my little Jenny, who's proper bad with the fever. She must have been sickening with it that night as you fetched her to the tree. Mr. Curzon seems like a parson, and doctor, and nurse, all in one. He come'd here late last night, and he took her temperature ready to tell the doctor this morning, and he's round here again now; and it's not as though he favours mine more than another's. He's just the same to every one who's bad."

H. Louisa Bedford

And what one said all said, and Paul pondered on their words. May Webster had spoken truly when she said that this man lived in the hearts of his people. Sally delayed her departure for London for a few weeks when she found that she could be of great service in the village by going and lending a helping hand when the mothers got overdone with nursing, for it was chiefly among the children of the place that the fever found its victims. Twenty succumbed, and then there was a day or two when no fresh case was reported.

Paul met the rector one morning and stayed to congratulate him on the fact that the fever seemed to have run its course, that there had been no death from it during the last few days, and apparently no fresh cases.

"Poor little Jenny Weldon passed away this morning; I was with her when she died," said the rector. Then came a long pause, and he cleared his throat. "My Kitty was the last case; she was pronounced to have the fever last night."

"Kitty!" echoed Paul, with a face almost as white as Mr. Curzon's own. "Good Heavens! and I was the double-dyed idiot who brought that child Jenny Weldon to the treat. Kitty probably caught it from her."

"That is quite impossible to decide," said Mr. Curzon, with a sad little smile; "the outbreak has been almost simultaneous. But Kitty's life is in God's Hands."

Paul turned away with an impatient exclamation; he had no word of comfort to offer, for he had but little hope that a child so delicate as Kitty would recover.

"If Sally could help in the nursing of her, or I in fetching any delicacy the child could fancy, you know we are ready to help," he said.

"Thank you; you have always been good to her."

It was a feeble fight that little Kitty made for life, and did not last many days. She had brief intervals of consciousness when she recognized the father, who was never absent from her bedside except when he visited the other sick children of his flock. All day long the rectory was besieged by anxious inquiries for Kitty, who was better known and more loved than any other child in the place; and Paul came each day with some offering of fruit or flowers. But before the week was over the passing-bell rang out, and a thrill of sympathy ran through the village, and the neighbours looked into each other's faces, and their kind eyes filled with tears as they said—

"That's little Miss Kitty gone home."

It was the phrase Mrs. Macdonald used as she brought in the breakfast for Paul and Sally that morning, and the tears ran down her cheeks as she said it.

"There may be some mistake, Mrs. Macdonald," said Paul, gently. "There are other children ill in the place besides Kitty."

"No, sir; it's true enough. My John got up in the dark and went to ask for her; and he saw the nurse, who told him she was dying then. She could not last the hour."

"And the rector?" inquired Sally, who was crying quietly. "Did she mention him?"

"Miss Kitty lay in his arms, poor lamb! He's never had his clothes off since she was taken ill, and he would not let her be frightened; he'd hold her fast until He came to fetch her," said Mrs. Macdonald, with simple conviction that the Good

H. Louisa Bedford

Shepherd Himself would lift little Kitty straight from her father's arms into His own.

Late that afternoon Paul called at the rectory to leave a wreath of white flowers from Sally and a bunch of arums from himself; and the rector, who saw him pass the study window, opened the door to him.

"I've only brought a few flowers from Sally and me," said Paul, omitting the usual greeting.

Mr. Curzon looked down at them for a moment, fingering the card attached to Paul's spray with hands that trembled. On it was written "For Kitty, from one who loved her."

"Thank you," he answered with a smile that was more pathetic than tears. "She loved you, too, very dearly. Will you give her them yourself?"

But Paul drew back with a shiver.

"Oh no; her bright, living face is the memory that I would have of her."

So it was the rector who carried up the flowers to the room where Kitty lay, and placed the wreath at her feet; and the arums framed the sweet, smiling face, and the card with its message of love was laid upon her breast, with the murmured prayer that the one who loved Kitty might learn to love Kitty's God.

All the villagers that were able attended Kitty's funeral two days later, drawn there by love and sympathy. Paul was there with Sally, sitting down in the belfry, close to the spot where Kitty's carriage had been placed upon the only other occasion when Paul had attended a service in Rudham church.

"If there is any meaning at all in the service, it is appropriate for Kitty," was the reason he had assigned to Sally for accompanying her. It seemed like a beautiful dream to him: the church nearly filled with people, the fragrance of the flowers as the little white coffin was carried into church headed by the rector and the choir, who sang, as they led the way to the chancel, the words of a hymn quite unfamiliar to Paul, and a few lines of which sounded clearly in his ears as they passed him.

"Death will be to slumber
In that sweet embrace,
And we shall awaken
To behold His Face."

Only one person followed the little coffin, and that was the nurse, who had loved Kitty as devotedly as any mother. The door behind Paul was gently pushed open after the service had begun, and he was vividly conscious of the presence of the woman he loved the best in the world—May Webster. She was dressed in black, and sank upon her knees by Sally's side. The intense sympathy of her expression made her look more beautiful than ever, giving the touch of softness that her features sometimes lacked. Throughout the service the rector's brave, strong voice never faltered, and it rose and fell with the others in Psalm and hymn. He seemed, for the time being, borne aloft upon the wings of faith and love; but when, the service ended, Paul made his way back to the church to fetch his hat, which he had accidently left behind him, he caught a glimpse of a white-robed figure prostrate before the altar, and the frame was convulsed with sobs. Nature must have her way; and not even the rector could at once bring his will into perfect submission with the will of God. His darling was taken from his sight, and his heart was aching over the dreary years that might intervene before he could see her again. There was a lump in Paul's throat as he noiselessly left the church. May and Sally waited for him.

"It's heart-breaking," said May, putting her hand into his. "I was bound to come."

"You return to London to-night, I suppose? You will come and have tea with us on your way, won't you?" said Sally, eagerly.

"I will come to tea. But I am not going back at present; I told mother I should stay down here for a little while, until all this trouble had passed away; it cannot be right that we should be doing nothing to help. I only wish I had come in time to see that little girl alive again."

Sally had moved away to help to arrange the flowers on the newly-filled-in grave, and Paul stood a little apart by May's side.

"I'm sorry for every one," said May. "It is almost enough to kill Mr. Curzon. And I have thought of you too; I was sorry for the loss of your one friend."

"Yes," said Paul. "I've been sorry for myself; I did not believe any child's death could affect me so deeply. Life is an unanswerable riddle from beginning to end."

"Unless the rector is right," said May, softly. "In which case we may find the answer on the other side."

Never had May appeared so beautiful or gracious as that evening when she sat listening to the story of all that had occurred in Rudham since she and her mother had gone to London.

"I'm so glad to be back," she said. "Mother thinks me

half-crazed for coming, and threw a dozen obstacles in my way. But I've brought Rose Lancaster with me, and the servants who are left in charge can manage for us; and, as for carriages it will do me good to walk for a little bit."

Paul left the talk almost entirely to the two girls; it was enough for him to sit and watch the play of May's beautiful features, and hear the sound of her voice. What could this sudden return of hers mean, he wondered? Was it a passing whim, or was it?—He left even the thought unfinished, and called himself a presumptuous fool!

The next morning he received a note from the rector asking him to call.

"There is a matter of extreme importance that I cannot decide until I have seen you, so will you kindly look in this evening?" he wrote.

Paul found him in his study, and noticed that the handsome face was thinner, and the dark lines under the eyes betrayed the suffering through which he had passed.

"I wanted you to come for many reasons," he said, pushing an easy-chair near to the fire. "To thank you, first of all, for the kindness you have poured on my Kitty from the day of your coming until now. There are not many men who would have taken so much trouble about a delicate little girl."

"You need not thank me," Paul answered with tears in his eyes. "She was a friend I shall sorely miss."

"And there is this letter I wish to show you," continued the rector, not daring to talk further of Kitty.

It was a letter from the Bishop of the diocese, suggesting that

Mr. Curzon should accept the living of Norrington, a populous town some thirty miles away. In money value it was less than Rudham, but "the needs of the place are great," wrote the Bishop. "You are in the heyday of your strength, and I believe you to be the man for the place. Unless there be any very urgent reason for your refusing to move, I greatly wish you to undertake it."

"Why can't the Bishop let well alone?" said Paul, as he returned the letter. "Of course, you will not go. I don't pretend to constitute myself a judge of a clergyman's work, but I should say that you have this place as well in hand as any man could. To move you, will be equal loss to yourself and Rudham."

"I cannot decide it so quickly. I do not believe in things happening by chance," said Mr. Curzon. "This letter came the day that Kitty passed away, and I telegraphed to the Bishop that I could decide nothing for a day or two; the one urgent reason that would have kept me here is gone, you see."

"Kitty?" questioned Paul.

"Yes; I could not have taken her to live in the heart of a town."

"Then you really had decided to leave us before you wrote to me."

"Several things point to it: a less strong man than I could undertake the work here. If it is God's voice that calls, I would not disobey it. One thought holds me back. What will happen here? Is it impertinent to ask? The presentation to the living is yours."

Paul smiled involuntarily. "And you scarcely think me the man to appoint to a cure of souls. I confess I don't myself feel I know enough about it. I should do as my godfather did before me, hand over the nomination of a successor to the Bishop. I believe this offer jumps with your own inclination."

"Only for one thing," said the rector, quietly, "that my house is 'left unto me desolate.'"

"And yet you call the God, who took your Kitty from you, a God of love."

"Yes. Who, looking at her pitiful little frame, can doubt it? My selfish heart cries out for her yet; but what could her life have been but one of constant suffering."

"But, I suppose, she was born like that?" said Paul, more to himself than to the rector.

Mr. Curzon's face twitched a little. "Oh no; she was the brightest, healthiest little child you have ever seen; and then she was dropped. And the girl who dropped her did not tell any one about it for months after—not until the child's back began to grow out."

"How did you find it out at last?" asked Paul, deeply interested.

"The girl came of her own accord to confess it. She was pretty well heart-broken when she discovered that Kitty was injured for life."

"I would never have forgiven her!" said Paul, bitterly.

"Yes, you would. You would have done much as I did, I

expect; I let her work out her repentance. She is the nurse who has devoted herself to Kitty like a mother, and who mourns for her like one, too. We can never be separated; where I go she will go. And now she has not Kitty she will help me to look after some of the sick children in my parish."

"So you have decided to go?"

"Yes; I think I have scarcely a choice in the matter."

The Vicar was not one to keep his people long in ignorance of a decision which affected both him and them so largely, and, on the following Sunday morning, he told them in a few words that he must leave them.

"Dear people," he said, "the decision has been sharp and sudden, and the pain of it still lingers in my heart as I talk to you to-day; but I dare not have it otherwise lest, in hesitating, my will should cross the will of God, for, as soldiers must obey the command of their captain, nor ask the reason why, so I, Christ's soldier and servant, must be ready at His Word to pass on to where the battle is most fierce, and where, maybe, the army needs reinforcement. Shall I be less brave than Abraham, who, at the call of God, left home and kindred to settle in a strange land amongst an alien people? Dear friends, as clearly as God's message came to Abraham in those far-off days, it has seemed to come to me, telling me to leave the home and people that I love, and to go, work for Him in another part of His vineyard. Therefore I obey."

There were tears on the upturned faces that listened, and, when the people left the church, there was an almost universal wail of lamentation. But reticent natures like the Macdonalds could find no relief in words; they walked silently side by side with tears in their eyes and an untold aching in their hearts.

"Life won't be the same again, John; we shan't get another like the good man," said Mrs. Macdonald, as they neared home.

"No," said John, slowly. "But if he don't make a fuss about it, no more won't we; he's sure about the call, and he dursn't disobey. But now we'll save for the collectin'!"

"What collectin'?"

"They'll make him a present. They are sure to make him a present; and we'll be ready when they call," said John.

But, with all his brave words, John's dinner was pushed away untouched, and his broad back was turned resolutely to his wife so that she might not guess that he was crying!

H. Louisa Bedford

CHAPTER XIV

A CHANGE OF MIND

Three months later Paul Lessing stood, one morning in March, with his hands thrust deep into his pockets, looking out of his sitting-room window. His eyes rested on the little plot of ground before him, with its borders of snowdrops and crocuses, and the road beyond, along which the village children in their scarlet cloaks hurried to school: a narrow boundary to a narrow life, he told himself—and lonely, since Sally had left him a week or two ago. He was intolerably dull, and Sally's letter, which lay open on the table, brimful as it was of new energies and interests, had set him wondering whether he could continue his present course of life much longer. There was positively no one left in the village, at present, with whom he could interchange an idea.

Mr. Curzon, with whom, in the last three months, he had become fairly intimate, had gone to his new field of work, leaving a blank behind him in every house in the place; his successor had not yet arrived. "And we are not likely to have much in common when he does come," Paul thought, with a smile. May Webster, after manfully fulfilling her purpose of helping in the village until the trouble and distress, brought by the fever, had passed away, had returned to London; and it was little enough that Paul had seen of her whilst she had been there. And that very day Paul had received a letter from Mrs. Webster to tell him that at Michaelmas she wished to vacate the Court, which she now kept on as a yearly tenant.

"It cannot matter to me," Paul said to himself. "In many ways, of course, it is the best thing that could happen." And yet he found himself thinking of nothing but the utter desolation of Rudham, when May's bright presence should be removed from it, when he could no longer hope for a passing glimpse of her in the street.

"I have vegetated down here until I run a risk of softening of the brain," he said aloud. "I must have change. I'll be off to London for a week, put up at my club, see a few of my friends, and unearth Sally in her new quarters."

The thought had scarcely formed itself before he began to carry it into execution: putting together his papers, looking out a convenient train. And, shoving his head inside the door of the Macdonald's sitting-room, he enlisted Mrs. Macdonald's help in the matter of packing.

"Rather sudden, sir, isn't it?" she said, as she knelt upon the floor in the centre of the clothes which Paul had pulled out of his drawers and littered about in hopeless confusion. "It's bad enough to lose Miss Sally, but John and I won't know ourselves when you've gone too."

"It won't be for very long," said Paul, good-humouredly, grateful to discover that anybody would miss him, and careful to suppress the fact that he was dull.

Arrived in London the stir and bustle of the streets was as refreshing to him as water to a thirsty man, and to find himself once more amongst his fellows in the club, where many a man greeted him with a friendly nod, was simply

H. Louisa Bedford

delightful, One friend asked him to dinner that night, another made an appointment for the play on the night following; his presence was demanded at an important political meeting, where he was requested to speak on the labour question. And again the thought forced itself upon him how much better he felt fitted to cope with the masses, and work at the big social problems of the day, than to deal with the individual lives of the people of Rudham. And the parliamentary career for which he longed was absolutely within his grasp, for a seat belonging to his political party was to be vacated in the autumn, and his name was already mentioned as that of the likely candidate; but there was no course open to him but to refuse the offer if it came. It took more means than he had at his disposal to do his duty by Rudham.

He found Sally keen and happy over her work, and was satisfied that she had discovered her proper vocation.

The last day of his London visit had come, and, late in the afternoon, Paul found himself walking down Park Lane; and he hesitated for a moment, when he came to the house which he knew to be the Websters, wondering whether he would call and answer Mrs. Webster's note in person. That, at any rate, would be the ostensible reason for his visit; he scarcely cared to admit that it was the longing for a sight of May's face that made it impossible for him to pass the door. In another minute he had mounted the steps and rung the bell, and was handed into a room crammed with people—society people, all talking society gossip over their tea. Many of them bestowed a passing glance upon Paul as he made his way towards Mrs. Webster, but their interest died down when they discovered that he was not of their set.

"Mr. Lessing!" exclaimed Mrs. Webster. "Quite a welcome surprise! You are not often in London, are you? So good of you to call. Have you had any tea? Yes? Pray have some more."

Then another visitor demanded her attention, and Paul found himself stranded in a room full of people of whom he knew not one. May was nowhere to be seen; but, as Paul sidled his way past chairs and tables, making for the door, he found himself face to face with her as she led a party of people from the conservatory back to the drawing-room. She was talking with that brilliant, rapid fluency which had marked the earlier stages of their acquaintance; but at sight of him she coloured and stretched out her hand with unmistakable cordiality.

"This is indeed an unexpected honour," she said, letting her other guests move on, and taking up her own position by Paul. "I should not have thought wild horses would have dragged you to a tea-fight."

"And they would not have done," Paul answered, with a laugh, "had I known that such a thing was in process; but, finding myself in London, I came to call in answer to a note of your mother's."

A professional singer at the far end of the room rose preparatory to singing, and May gave an impatient little exclamation.

"Come into the conservatory and talk; I'm tired of all these people. You bring a whiff of country air with you."

As she spoke she led the way towards two easy-chairs, placed by the fountain in the middle of the conservatory, and, sinking into one herself, she motioned Paul to the other. From the half-open door of the drawing-room came the confused murmur of voices, dominated by the tenor soloist; but to Paul that society life seemed miles distant. He was enfolded by a sense of enchantment: for him, at that moment, there was but two people in the world—himself and May. To speak would be to break the brief spell of enjoyment, so he sat silent and content.

"We are wasting the time; I brought you here to talk," said May, turning towards him with a smile. "How do things fare at Rudham now Mr. Curzon has gone?"

"Badly; there is a sense of flatness. He embodied the life of the village in a way one could not believe unless one had lived there. I've seen a lot of him in the last few months; we were fairly driven into each other's society."

"How do you get on together?"

"To know Curzon intimately goes halfway towards converting one to his way of thinking," said Paul, slowly.

May looked up quickly.

"I don't mean that I am fully prepared to accept his opinions, but I have modified my views concerning them," Paul went on. "A man like Curzon, and his enormous power for good, cannot be ignored. His creed, which makes him what he is, must be reckoned with as a motive-force in the world. I said to myself at one time that, starting from opposite poles, he and I worked for the same end—the good of the race. But where I seem only to scratch the surface, he gets below it. Look at Burney, for example. I believed I had made a man of him by restoring his self-respect and giving him a fresh chance—by trusting him, in fact. It did well enough for a time, but then he broke out worse than ever. Then, from what Tom told me, Curzon stepped in, saved him from suicide, and saved him from himself; and has given him, apparently, some principle to live by that will turn him into a fine character yet—at any rate, I get excellent accounts of him."

"I did not know he had tried to kill himself," said May; "perhaps that is what has sobered poor Rose Lancaster so effectually. She told me the other day that she would marry no one but Tom. By the way, what brought you to London?"

"Mixed motives. Sheer dulness for one thing."

"You once aired a theory that only stupid people could be dull."

"Then, I suppose, I have grown stupid; I have not enough to occupy me, for one thing. If I could carry out all my whims I could be busy enough; but I have had to abandon that scheme for rebuilding a good many of my cottages from want of money, and that same want stands between me and my one ambition: a seat in Parliament. I might have had a chance of a vacancy in the autumn. By the way, as you intend to throw me over, I trust that amongst your numerous friends you will find me another tenant for the Court."

"I don't understand what you are talking of! Who is going to throw you over?"

"Your mother has written to say that she wishes to leave at Michaelmas. Her letter was my excuse for calling."

May did not answer for a minute; she was busily pondering what her mother's reason could have been for arriving at this decision without consulting her. It might be that the relations between themselves and the Blands being somewhat strained, she had thought it wise to go somewhere else, or—and here May's heart quickened its beating—it might be that she feared a rival in Paul Lessing.

"I hope you are sorry to lose us," she said.

"Am I to tell the conventional falsehood or the truth?" Paul asked.

"The truth, of course; we have not studied conventionality much, have we?"

"Then I am unfeignedly glad," said Paul, deliberately.

May had turned rather white. "You don't mince matters certainly."

"No, I don't; but I prefer solitude to living perpetually within sight of unattainable happiness. Our friendship is destroyed, you remember; you admitted as much once. I cannot pretend that you are an ordinary acquaintance, and, therefore, to have you taken out of my reach is really the best thing that could happen to me."

"And you have left any wish I might have about it outside your calculation," said May.

"It cannot signify to you where you live. You will amuse yourself wherever you are."

"It signifies considerably; as I like Rudham, at present, better than any place in the world."

Paul broke into an incredulous laugh.

"I suppose it would be an impertinence to ask your reason for this unaccountable preference?"

"It is a simple one: you live there," said May, with averted face.

Paul sprang to his feet and stood before May with arms folded, and looked down at her with eyes that literally burned.

"May!" he said hoarsely, "if it is a joke it is a cruel one."

"Oh, it's true that you have grown stupid!" cried May, between laughter and tears. "It is no joke to have to tell you that I have changed my mind. I love you better than all the world besides."

With an incoherent cry Paul clasped her to his breast.

"My darling! my darling!" he said, after the rapture of that first moment, "I am not worthy, and the sacrifice on your side is too great. I had no right ever to ask you to marry me. What will the world say of me? I could wish that you had no fortune—"

"Oh, nonsense! you were groaning for want of it just now. It is my own, to do as I like with; and I shall have a lot more, some day, unless mother disinherits me."

"Which reminds me that I have to face her," said Paul, rather ruefully.

"I think you had better go at once," said May, with merry decision, "and leave mother to me. I don't pretend she will like it; but she may consent, as she has been grievously worried by the fear that I was going to be an old maid—and so I should have been but for you."

Paul tried to repossess himself of her hands, but May had glided back to the drawing-room, turning as she left to tell him to call again in the morning. Left to himself, Paul tried to collect his thoughts, and to realize the intense happiness

H. Louisa Bedford

that had come to him. If it were true that May loved him, he would marry her in the face of all opposition, for she knew well enough that he did not care for her money, but for herself. Then he fell again to wondering whether she had sufficiently counted the cost of uniting her life with his, for, in marrying, Paul felt it would be impossible for him to change the whole scheme of his life. His objects and ambitions would be the same after it as before, and, unless May was prepared to share them, they would gradually drift apart. He must put it all before her to-morrow, lest she should make a lifelong mistake.

But May had made no mistake; she knew her own mind, at last, for absence from Paul had taught it her. She had turned with absolute loathing from the mill-round of gaiety which was the only marked characteristic of her life in London; and her thoughts had recurred persistently to Rudham, until finally, in the time of distress, she had followed the dictates of her heart and gone down there. But not until the day of Kitty's funeral, when she stood beside Paul at her grave, had she owned to herself that he was the man she loved: a conviction which deepened into certainty in the weeks which followed, for, although she saw little of him, to be in the place where he lived, and in some way to share his work, made her happy, and gave her a sense of repose which had not been hers since she left.

Mrs. Webster shed some very bitter tears when, after dinner that evening, May announced her engagement.

"It is wicked of him to have asked you! he is as poor as a church mouse!"

"I can't remember, exactly, but I don't think he did ask me," said May, knitting her pretty brows. "He did once before, but I don't think he did to-day. But he was so very miserable that—"

"Well!" interposed Mrs. Webster, "in my young days girls left it to the men to speak."

"Oh, mother, don't scold! I am so happy—happier that I have ever been before. You know you have wished me to marry; let me marry the man I love."

"It is such an ill-assorted match; he has no money—"

"And I have plenty," said May.

"And how can I ever consent to your living in a cottage?" went on Mrs. Webster, with a wail of despair.

"Oh, we have not come to that yet!" May answered, unable to check a laugh; "but I dare say he will not wish it. We could live quite simply at the Court. I wonder if we shall run to a house-parlourmaid?"

"It's no laughing matter; you have been used to every luxury, May."

"I have had more than my share. I feel rather a surfeit of the sweetest things."

"And he does not go to church—"

"But he is more in earnest than many of the men who do," said May. "Of this I am sure, that he is seeking after God; if I were not sure, I do not believe I should have the courage to marry him. A year back I should not have cared what a man thought as long as he led a straight life, but lately I have felt different about things. My own convictions are stronger."

H. Louisa Bedford

"Well, if we discuss it from now until Doomsday I shall not like it, May; but it is equally certain that if you have set your mind on this man you will not give him up."

"I have set my heart upon him," said May, an unusual softness in her voice. "After all, mother, love is the first thing."

Mrs. Webster sat silent, the tears dropping down her face. Love, either of God or man, had been no important factor in her life. She had married for money, and such love as she could give had been centred on her one beautiful daughter; but even with her, her ambition was stronger than her love, and it received its deathblow with May's unaccountable choice of a husband. Further opposition she saw to be useless, so she surrendered with as good a grace as possible.

When May's engagement was publicly announced friends poured in to offer congratulations that had a note of surprise behind them; but Mrs. Webster proved fully equal to the occasion.

"Yes," she said; "May has been a long time making her choice, and now it seems a funny one, doesn't it? But Mr. Lessing is a very clever man, and May became bitten with his views first, and with the propounder of them afterwards. He is the sort of man who will make a career for himself yet. I believe he means to stand for—in the autumn."

Perhaps no one received the news with such genuine delight as Sally, who came flying up to Park Lane directly she heard of it.

"I've always thought Paul the nicest man in the world, and you the most fascinating woman; and that you should make a match of it is ideally delightful," she said. "It really is very funny, though, when I come to think of it, and look back at that night in Brussels."

"What about that night at Brussels?" asked Paul, who had entered the room unperceived by either of the girls. But Sally laughed and held her tongue.

"If you had stayed away a minute longer I should have wormed the truth out of the too-truthful Sally," May said, turning upon him with a smile. "You clearly hated me."

"I don't think I ever hated you. I believe I struggled from the first against a tremendous fascination that you possessed for me. I quarrelled with your surroundings, with your money rather than with you."

"It is a distinct judgment that that same money will enable you to carry out all your schemes," May said quaintly, "from the new cottages to the seat in Parliament."

"I shall wish you to do exactly what you like, May."

"And what else could give me so much pleasure?"

"Oh, May, how perfectly lovely it all sounds!" cried Sally, enthusiastically. "And shall you have open-air evenings on the bowling-green for the village people, with a band playing and every one dancing? If so, ask me down with a contingent of girls."

When Paul returned to Rudham and informed Mrs. Macdonald of his approaching marriage, he was a little puzzled by the look of alarm with which she received the news.

"Come, come, Mrs. Macdonald! you have been as good as a

mother to me; I thought you would be the first to wish me good luck," Paul said.

"It's not that, sir! it's not that at all, that I'm thinking; but plain people like John and me could noways manage for a pretty lady like Miss Webster," she said.

Paul sat down and laughed. "So that's it. Well! I had not thought of bringing my wife here to live. Happy as you have made me, it would be a little small for her. I suppose we shall go to the Court, and I could turn my rooms here into a workman's club, couldn't I? And we could keep a bedroom for any of Miss Sally's girls who want a change."

After which Mrs. Macdonald recovered her spirits, and offered her congratulations with Scotch sincerity.

"She's bonny, sir! she's very bonny! But my John will say that there's not another lady in the world like our Miss Sally. His heart is set on her, that it is! And when will be the wedding, if I may be so bold as to ask?"

"To-morrow, if I had *my* way. Six weeks hence, as I have to wait Miss Webster's pleasure; and, I believe, in the years to come, she will rival Miss Sally in your affections."

"Maybe, sir," replied Mrs. Macdonald, cautiously.

* * * * * *

More than two years had passed; and on a sunny day in June, Rose Lancaster was once again making her way across the bowling-green at the Court towards the rose-garden, bent upon the same quest as on the summer morning, which seemed such a long time ago, when Tom Burney had first declared his love for her. It was said in the village that Rose had lost her looks, and certainly the indefinable first blush of youth had faded; but if Rose's face had lost its delicacy of colouring, it had gained infinitely in expression. The blue eyes were soft and wistful, the pretty lips had lost their trick of pouting, the head was poised less saucily; trouble had taught Rose lessons which had left a lasting impression upon her character. She had been retained in Mrs. Lessing's service; nor ever showed any desire to quit it, until such time as Tom was ready to come home and fetch her. But oh! how long it seemed to wait. He had hinted, a month or two back, at the possibility of his being sent over to England upon his master's business; but in the letter which followed immediately after, no mention had been made of the subject, so Rose feared that the happy chance was not to come yet, since which time there had been silence—the longest silence that had occurred since Tom had left. Whether the rose-garden unconsciously brought back her lover to her mind it is impossible to say, but as Rose snipped the buds there were tears in her eyes with the simple longing for news of her absent lover. She chose all white roses to-day, for the newly-arrived baby-girl at the Court was to be baptized, and Mr. Curzon was coming to take the service; and Rose had planned that she would slip off quietly to the church and put a wreath of white roses round the font. It was a business that must be carried through with secrecy and despatch, as presently her mistress would want her to help her to dress: she was far from strong yet. A straying bramble caught her gown and held it fast, and with an impatient little cry she stooped down to disentangle it, when, to her astonishment, a great brown hand from behind closed upon hers, and a strong arm was slipped round her waist, and a voice, that set her trembling from head to foot, exclaimed—

"Rose, Rose, my beauty! what luck to find you, the first minute I've come, like this! I was just making my way up the drive, and caught sight of something shining through the trees; and if it wasn't your head shining all yellow in the sun the same as when I left it! And I crept up behind you, and caught you crying over a thorn, I do believe."

Needless to say it was Tom Burney who was the speaker, a broader, bigger Tom than Rose remembered: a handsome, strong fellow that any girl might be proud of as a lover, who spoke half in jest to hide the fact that tears were not far from his own eyes. He held her so tightly clasped to his breast, that it was some few minutes before Rose could either speak or get a good look at her lover.

"Oh, Tom, you've taken the life out of me; you've given me such a start!" she said when she could speak. "How brown and big you are!—but you're worth the waiting for. Oh dear, how glad I am you've come!" And then Rose began to sob helplessly, and needed a deal of comforting, which Tom was not slow to offer. "There!" said Rose, at last, pushing him from her, and showing him her dimples for the first time, "you are wasting all my time; but you can come down to the church, if you like, and help me to put the roses on the font."

"What for?" asked Tom, unsympathetically, preferring the privacy of the rose-garden.

"For little Miss Kitty as is to be; that's the new baby at the Court. And nothing will satisfy Mr. Lessing but that she shall be named after the one that's gone. Mr. Curzon is coming to baptize her."

"Is he?" cried Tom, eagerly. "I'll come, then, and wait all day for a sight of him, the best friend I've ever had, Rose, my darling. Shall I ask him to tie up you and me?"

"Oh!" cried Rose, blushing rosy red, "I had not thought of that yet, Tom."

"Time you did," said Tom. "I must start back again in a month, and I'm not going without you."

"Oh no," said Rose. "It seems to come sudden at the last, but I've waited so long that I'll come when you like. I've not looked at another man since you went away."

Tom caught her again and kissed her. "And there was plenty to look at you, I'll bet."

"Yes, plenty," Rose admitted, with a dash of her old coquetry.

Then hand in hand, like two happy children, they walked down the lane to the church; and Tom stood and handed the flowers, which Rose's deft fingers arranged round the font. And all that miserable past seemed blotted out, and a future of perfect happiness seemed opening out before them. Just as their task was finished, and they stood side by side admiring their handiwork, the church door was softly pushed open, and Mr. Curzon entered. Real joy flashed into his face as he recognized Tom Burney, and saw that Rose was with him; but the words of greeting were very simple.

"So you've come home, Tom?" he said, as he heartily grasped his hand.

"For a bit, sir—just for a week or two."

"And you will take out Rose with you, I expect?" with a kindly smile at the pretty, downcast head.

"Well, yes, sir; that is my meaning. And we were thinking, she and I, as we would not feel rightly married unless you was kind enough to come and marry us."

H. Louisa Bedford

"And that I will gladly."

"You're the best friend as ever I had," said Tom speaking with some effort. "And if I've kept straight and got a good name, it's you I have to thank for it."

"No, no," said Mr. Curzon; "God alone could do that. I may have chanced to be the sign-post that directed you to Him. Shall we thank Him now for bringing you back, and pray that He may bless your life with Rose?"

So side by side the three knelt down, and in a few simple words Mr. Curzon commended them to God. And when he rose from his knees he laid his hands upon their heads in blessing.

Then Tom and Rose made their way back to the Court, sobered, but unspeakably happy, whilst Mr. Curzon lingered awhile by Kitty's grave.

"There's to be another little Kitty named in memory of you, my darling," he said aloud, as he turned away from the grave with a tender smile on his face.

It never seemed to him that his own little Kitty was far from him, and a prayer was in his heart that Kitty the second might be as sweet, as good as the one who was ever present in his thoughts.

Paul Lessing, too, thought tenderly of his first child-friend that same afternoon, as he stood a little apart from the group gathered round the font, and heard the familiar name of Kitty bestowed upon his own little child. That first Kitty had been dear to him, but the baby who whimpered in Mr. Curzon's arms was nearer still and dearer; and in the full realization of his own fatherhood Paul knelt, and, with his face hidden in his hands, acknowledged the Fatherhood of God.

There was a very large party at the Court, that evening, to which every inhabitant of Rudham had received an invitation —an invitation printed in silver letters on a very small card.

"Kitty Lessing requests the company of Mr. and Mrs.—, etc."

It had been May's particular wish that the invitations should be issued in her daughter's name, and Paul, who considered the notion a little fantastic, had yielded to his wife's whim.

"It seems rather nonsense that the giver of the feast should be fast asleep in her cradle upstairs," he said, when he found himself standing by Mr. Curzon in the course of the evening, "but May would have it so."

The two men stood side by side upon the terrace, looking down upon the moving crowd of happy people that wandered hither and thither about the beautiful grounds. From the bowling-green below there floated the strains of a string-band specially hired for the occasion; but, above it all, came the sound of Sally's laughter as she tried to steer some of the village boys and girls safely through the mysteries of a new country dance—an effort not wholly crowned with success. The shifting scene was full of animation and happiness.

"I think Mrs. Lessing was right," said Mr. Curzon, presently. "Kitty is promising, by proxy, that she will carry on the work of kindliness and good-will that you and your wife have begun in Rudham."

"I'm glad you are on my side," said May, who had come up in time to hear Mr. Curzon's words. "We'll have a birthday party every year as long as Kitty lives at home. I came to find you, Paul; some of the elderly ones are going, and I want you to be at the gate to say good-bye."

"No, no," Paul answered; "we'll go together to the bowling-green and issue a yearly invitation."

A few minutes later Paul stood bare-headed, with May by his side, upon the band-stand; and the guests from all parts of the grounds gathered round, feeling that the squire had something to say to them.

"My friends," Paul began, "I am here not to make a speech, but just to tell you, quite simply, what great pleasure it has given my wife and myself to see you here this evening, at the birthday party of our little girl. If she be spared to us it is our wish that every birthday of hers should be celebrated in a similar manner. Her name, I hope, will bring back to your memory the thought of another Kitty, who lived long enough to make her influence felt in every cottage of our village. That our little daughter shall also find a place in your hearts is her mother's and my chief ambition concerning her."

There was a moment's pause when Paul ceased speaking, a passing hesitation lest any open manifestation of gladness over the birthday festival of the new Kitty should make their late rector more painfully conscious of the loss of his own little daughter; and with his quick, intuitive sympathy Mr. Curzon understood and appreciated the momentary silence. He sprang on to the platform and took his place by Paul's side.

"Give expression to your thanks in the way which our entertainers will like the best," he said. "Three cheers for Kitty Lessing!"

The sound of the hearty cheering reached even to the

nursery, and baby Kitty stirred for a moment, opened her dark eyes, then, turning her head on the pillow, slept more profoundly than ever.

In years to come she would be told the tale of her first birthday party.

THE END

H. Louisa Bedford

Choose from Thousands of 1stWorldLibrary Classics By

A. M. Barnard
Ada Leverson
Adolphus William Ward
Aesop
Agatha Christie
Alexander Aaronsohn
Alexander Kielland
Alexandre Dumas
Alfred Gatty
Alfred Ollivant
Alice Duer Miller
Alice Turner Curtis
Alice Dunbar
Allen Chapman
Alleyne Ireland
Ambrose Bierce
Amelia E. Barr
Amory H. Bradford
Andrew Lang
Andrew McFarland Davis
Andy Adams
Angela Brazil
Anna Alice Chapin
Anna Sewell
Annie Besant
Annie Hamilton Donnell
Annie Payson Call
Annie Roe Carr
Annonaymous
Anton Chekhov
Archibald Lee Fletcher
Arnold Bennett
Arthur C. Benson
Arthur Conan Doyle
Arthur M. Winfield
Arthur Ransome
Arthur Schnitzler
Arthur Train
Atticus
B.H. Baden-Powell
B. M. Bower
B. C. Chatterjee
Baroness Emmuska Orczy
Baroness Orczy
Basil King
Bayard Taylor
Ben Macomber
Bertha Muzzy Bower
Bjornstjerne Bjornson

Booth Tarkington
Boyd Cable
Bram Stoker
C. Collodi
C. E. Orr
C. M. Ingleby
Carolyn Wells
Catherine Parr Traill
Charles A. Eastman
Charles Amory Beach
Charles Dickens
Charles Dudley Warner
Charles Farrar Browne
Charles Ives
Charles Kingsley
Charles Klein
Charles Hanson Towne
Charles Lathrop Pack
Charles Romyn Dake
Charles Whibley
Charles Willing Beale
Charlotte M. Braeme
Charlotte M. Yonge
Charlotte Perkins Stetson
Clair W. Hayes
Clarence Day Jr.
Clarence E. Mulford
Clemence Housman
Confucius
Coningsby Dawson
Cornelis DeWitt Wilcox
Cyril Burleigh
D. H. Lawrence
Daniel Defoe
David Garnett
Dinah Craik
Don Carlos Janes
Donald Keyhoe
Dorothy Kilner
Dougan Clark
Douglas Fairbanks
E. Nesbit
E. P. Roe
E. Phillips Oppenheim
E. S. Brooks
Earl Barnes
Edgar Rice Burroughs
Edith Van Dyne
Edith Wharton

Edward Everett Hale
Edward J. O'Biren
Edward S. Ellis
Edwin L. Arnold
Eleanor Atkins
Eleanor Hallowell Abbott
Eliot Gregory
Elizabeth Gaskell
Elizabeth McCracken
Elizabeth Von Arnim
Ellem Key
Emerson Hough
Emilie F. Carlen
Emily Bronte
Emily Dickinson
Enid Bagnold
Enilor Macartney Lane
Erasmus W. Jones
Ernie Howard Pie
Ethel May Dell
Ethel Turner
Ethel Watts Mumford
Eugene Sue
Eugenie Foa
Eugene Wood
Eustace Hale Ball
Evelyn Everett-green
Everard Cotes
F. H. Cheley
F. J. Cross
F. Marion Crawford
Fannie E. Newberry
Federick Austin Ogg
Ferdinand Ossendowski
Fergus Hume
Florence A. Kilpatrick
Fremont B. Deering
Francis Bacon
Francis Darwin
Frances Hodgson Burnett
Frances Parkinson Keyes
Frank Gee Patchin
Frank Harris
Frank Jewett Mather
Frank L. Packard
Frank V. Webster
Frederic Stewart Isham
Frederic Trevor Hill
Frederick Winslow Taylor

Friedrich Kerst
Friedrich Nietzsche
Fyodor Dostoyevsky
G.A. Henty
G.K. Chesterton
Gabrielle E. Jackson
Garrett P. Serviss
Gaston Leroux
George A. Warren
George Ade
Geroge Bernard Shaw
George Cary Eggleston
George Durston
George Ebers
George Eliot
George Gissing
George MacDonald
George Meredith
George Orwell
George Sylvester Viereck
George Tucker
George W. Cable
George Wharton James
Gertrude Atherton
Gordon Casserly
Grace E. King
Grace Gallatin
Grace Greenwood
Grant Allen
Guillermo A. Sherwell
Gulielma Zollinger
Gustav Flaubert
H. A. Cody
H. B. Irving
H. C. Bailey
H. G. Wells
H. H. Munro
H. Irving Hancock
H. R. Naylor
H. Rider Haggard
H. W. C. Davis
Haldeman Julius
Hall Caine
Hamilton Wright Mabie
Hans Christian Andersen
Harold Avery
Harold McGrath
Harriet Beecher Stowe
Harry Castlemon
Harry Coghill
Harry Houidini

Hayden Carruth
Helent Hunt Jackson
Helen Nicolay
Hendrik Conscience
Hendy David Thoreau
Henri Barbusse
Henrik Ibsen
Henry Adams
Henry Ford
Henry Frost
Henry James
Henry Jones Ford
Henry Seton Merriman
Henry W Longfellow
Herbert A. Giles
Herbert Carter
Herbert N. Casson
Herman Hesse
Hildegard G. Frey
Homer
Honore De Balzac
Horace B. Day
Horace Walpole
Horatio Alger Jr.
Howard Pyle
Howard R. Garis
Hugh Lofting
Hugh Walpole
Humphry Ward
Ian Maclaren
Inez Haynes Gillmore
Irving Bacheller
Isabel Cecilia Williams
Isabel Hornibrook
Israel Abrahams
Ivan Turgenev
J. G.Austin
J. Henri Fabre
J. M. Barrie
J. M. Walsh
J. Macdonald Oxley
J. R. Miller
J. S. Fletcher
J. S. Knowles
J. Storer Clouston
J. W. Duffield
Jack London
Jacob Abbott
James Allen
James Andrews
James Baldwin

James Branch Cabell
James DeMille
James Joyce
James Lane Allen
James Lane Allen
James Oliver Curwood
James Oppenheim
James Otis
James R. Driscoll
Jane Abbott
Jane Austen
Jane L. Stewart
Janet Aldridge
Jens Peter Jacobsen
Jerome K. Jerome
Jessie Graham Flower
John Buchan
John Burroughs
John Cournos
John F. Kennedy
John Gay
John Glasworthy
John Habberton
John Joy Bell
John Kendrick Bangs
John Milton
John Philip Sousa
John Taintor Foote
Jonas Lauritz Idemil Lie
Jonathan Swift
Joseph A. Altsheler
Joseph Carey
Joseph Conrad
Joseph E. Badger Jr
Joseph Hergesheimer
Joseph Jacobs
Jules Vernes
Julian Hawthrone
Julie A Lippmann
Justin Huntly McCarthy
Kakuzo Okakura
Karle Wilson Baker
Kate Chopin
Kenneth Grahame
Kenneth McGaffey
Kate Langley Bosher
Kate Langley Bosher
Katherine Cecil Thurston
Katherine Stokes
L. A. Abbot
L. T. Meade

L. Frank Baum
Latta Griswold
Laura Dent Crane
Laura Lee Hope
Laurence Housman
Lawrence Beasley
Leo Tolstoy
Leonid Andreyev
Lewis Carroll
Lewis Sperry Chafer
Lilian Bell
Lloyd Osbourne
Louis Hughes
Louis Joseph Vance
Louis Tracy
Louisa May Alcott
Lucy Fitch Perkins
Lucy Maud Montgomery
Luther Benson
Lydia Miller Middleton
Lyndon Orr
M. Corvus
M. H. Adams
Margaret E. Sangster
Margret Howth
Margaret Vandercook
Margaret W. Hungerford
Margret Penrose
Maria Edgeworth
Maria Thompson Daviess
Mariano Azuela
Marion Polk Angellotti
Mark Overton
Mark Twain
Mary Austin
Mary Catherine Crowley
Mary Cole
Mary Hastings Bradley
Mary Roberts Rinehart
Mary Rowlandson
M. Wollstonecraft Shelley
Maud Lindsay
Max Beerbohm
Myra Kelly
Nathaniel Hawthrone
Nicolo Machiavelli
O. F. Walton
Oscar Wilde
Owen Johnson
P.G. Wodehouse
Paul and Mabel Thorne

Paul G. Tomlinson
Paul Severing
Percy Brebner
Percy Keese Fitzhugh
Peter B. Kyne
Plato
Quincy Allen
R. Derby Holmes
R. L. Stevenson
R. S. Ball
Rabindranath Tagore
Rahul Alvares
Ralph Bonehill
Ralph Henry Barbour
Ralph Victor
Ralph Waldo Emmerson
Rene Descartes
Ray Cummings
Rex Beach
Rex E. Beach
Richard Harding Davis
Richard Jefferies
Richard Le Gallienne
Robert Barr
Robert Frost
Robert Gordon Anderson
Robert L. Drake
Robert Lansing
Robert Lynd
Robert Michael Ballantyne
Robert W. Chambers
Rosa Nouchette Carey
Rudyard Kipling
Saint Augustine
Samuel B. Allison
Samuel Hopkins Adams
Sarah Bernhardt
Sarah C. Hallowell
Selma Lagerlof
Sherwood Anderson
Sigmund Freud
Standish O'Grady
Stanley Weyman
Stella Benson
Stella M. Francis
Stephen Crane
Stewart Edward White
Stijn Streuvels
Swami Abhedananda
Swami Parmananda
T. S. Ackland

T. S. Arthur
The Princess Der Ling
Thomas A. Janvier
Thomas A Kempis
Thomas Anderton
Thomas Bailey Aldrich
Thomas Bulfinch
Thomas De Quincey
Thomas Dixon
Thomas H. Huxley
Thomas Hardy
Thomas More
Thornton W. Burgess
U. S. Grant
Upton Sinclair
Valentine Williams
Various Authors
Vaughan Kester
Victor Appleton
Victor G. Durham
Victoria Cross
Virginia Woolf
Wadsworth Camp
Walter Camp
Walter Scott
Washington Irving
Wilbur Lawton
Wilkie Collins
Willa Cather
Willard F. Baker
William Dean Howells
William le Queux
W. Makepeace Thackeray
William W. Walter
William Shakespeare
Winston Churchill
Yei Theodora Ozaki
Yogi Ramacharaka
Young E. Allison
Zane Grey

www.ingramcontent.com/pod-product-compliance
Lightning Source LLC
Chambersburg PA
CBHW030330180626
46810CB00003B/1296